THE EVOLUTION OF MANN

The Hal Leonard Jazz Biography Series

THE EVOLUTION OF MANN

Herbie Mann & the Flute in Jazz

CARY GINELL

With a Foreword by Hubert Laws

Hal Leonard Books

An Imprint of Hal Leonard Corporation

Published in 2014 by Hal Leonard Books
An Imprint of Hal Leonard Corporation
7777 West Bluemound Road
Milwaukee, WI 53213

Trade Book Division Editorial Offices
33 Plymouth St., Montclair, NJ 07042

Printed in the United States of America

Book design by Michael Kellner

Library of Congress Cataloging-in-Publication Data

Ginell, Cary.
 The evolution of Mann : Herbie Mann & the flute in jazz / Cary Ginell.
     pages cm. -- (Hal Leonard jazz biography series)
 Includes bibliographical references and index.
 ISBN 978-1-4584-1981-1 (pbk.)
 1. Mann, Herbie, 1930-2003. 2. Flute players--United States--Biography. 3. Jazz musicians--United States--Biography. I. Title.
 ML419.M234G56 2014
 788.3'2165092--dc23
 [B]
                                    2013050159

www.halleonardbooks.com

"My music is like a smorgasbord table. I listen to everything."
—HERBIE MANN

Contents

Recording in Rio de Janeiro, October 17, 1962. Courtesy of MCG Jazz.

Foreword
Hubert Laws

My introduction to Herbie Mann was during my high school years. A duo recording he did with Sam Most marked a distinct difference between the two---Herbie's style contrasted with Sam's bebop approach. I believe this led to Herbie's greater commercial success. I learned to highly respect his acute business acumen very early. The recognition of the flute in crossover fusion jazz can understandably be attributed to Herbie's commercial expansion. During my tenure with Mongo Santamaría, Herbie's appearance on the same bill revealed even more of that special prowess. His "Memphis Underground" recording had an indirect effect on the decision I made to leave the profitable David Frost TV show to sign with CTI Records, finally propelling the direction of my career. In his waning last months, we spoke often by phone as he maintained a positive spirit during his difficult health challenge. His legacy demands respect from every jazz flute player for putting our voice on the musical map.

Introduction
Cary Ginell

My interest in writing Herbie Mann's life story began in 1999, when I was writing and producing a radio documentary for National Public Radio's *Jazz Profiles* series. For that program, I flew to New Mexico and spent two days interviewing Herbie at his comfortable adobe home in Santa Fe. He greeted me in a gray sweat suit, looking healthy and content, although he had been fighting prostate cancer for three years. As a flute player myself, I told him how I tried playing along with "Memphis Underground" when I was in junior high school, which amused him. When I asked him for his advice on how to practice the flute, he said, "Play what you love. End of lesson."

Herbie was generous with his time that weekend, patiently and thoughtfully answering every question until I had exhausted my talking points. He then sent out to his favorite delicatessen for corned beef sandwiches, one of his more pedestrian culinary indulgences, left over from living his first sixty years in New York City. On the wall of his office was the original framed painting by Romanian artist Dimitrie Berea used on the cover of *The Inspiration I Feel*, Herbie's 1968 tribute to the music of Ray Charles. Herbie's flutes—a Haynes C flute and an Artley alto he had owned since 1955—stood at attention on a floor stand nearby.

After finishing our lunch, he picked up his flute and played a samba and a little of "Memphis Underground" to a recorded rhythm track and talked excitedly about his upcoming CD, *Eastern European Roots*, playing for me a digital tape of raw demos from the album. There was a sense of satisfied calm about him that weekend. He knew his cancer was inoperable, but didn't let it affect his demeanor or positive attitude toward life. We parted as friends, and I made a mental note that there was much more to his career than what we had discussed. I became convinced that, despite thirteen years of winning the *DownBeat* Readers Poll as jazz's favorite flutist, Herbie had not gotten the recognition he deserved as one of the most important and influential musicians in the history of jazz.

Herbie Mann did a lot of interviews during his fifty-year career, but one of his long-standing statements was that his goal in music was to be as synonymous on the flute as Benny Goodman was on the clarinet. He never had a "business plan" for how to achieve this lofty aspiration, but managed to do so by relying on one word: opportunity.

When Herbie Mann started playing jazz on the flute, he had few precedents to look to as he formulated a style. He might not have done anything more with the flute than what other reed players had done: use the instrument to double with. But in January 1953, the opportunity arose for him to play flute in Mat Mathews's accordion-led nightclub combo. From that point on, Herbie's career hopscotched from one "opportunity" to another. It appeared that chance encounters and inclinations drove his professional path, as he used his instinct and knack for business to make his decisions.

That, in addition to an innate restlessness, made him a nomadic presence in jazz throughout his life. To his fans, it was exciting, for they never knew where he was going to go next. To critics interested in the convenience of pigeonholing him as one kind of musician or another, it was frustrating. In many cases, they gave up on him altogether as he jumped from one musical style to another, crossing not just the continent but exploring world music as no other musician had done before.

Herbie Mann developed the ability to not only recognize opportunities when they arose, but also to perform and write music within a variety of musical and cultural styles while retaining his individuality as a performer. In getting to know Herbie toward the end of his life, I found he possessed a rare combination of passion, professionalism, business acumen, confidence, ego, and musical ability, but most of all, an insatiable curiosity, the combination of which enabled him to explore musical frontiers where no one before had thought of journeying.

Although Herbie was not the first jazz musician to play the flute, he was the first to specialize on the instrument. It was the versatility and pervasiveness of flutelike instruments in cultures all over the globe that allowed Herbie to begin exploring world music. Because of his efforts during the 1950s and '60s, no musician has been more instrumental in expanding jazz beyond American borders than he was.

He had a keen eye for talent, giving a seemingly endless list of musicians early opportunities to perform and record, including Chick Corea, Hubert Laws, Sonny Sharrock, Miroslav Vitouš, Roy Ayers, and Romero Lubambo. He was one of the first jazz musicians in the post--big band era to have commercial crossover success in the pop world—"opening the door," as he was fond of saying, to audiences beyond the comfort of the jazz nightclub scene of the fifties.

There are musicians who challenge Herbie's ability as a flutist. Herbie himself was modest about his own musicianship, but when it was showtime, few could generate as much excitement in a live performance as he did.

After serving as a New York sideman during the 1950s, Herbie exploded onto the national scene when he signed with Atlantic Records in 1960. During the next twenty years, he recorded dozens of albums in a dazzling spectrum of musical styles, including Afro-Cuban, Brazilian, Middle Eastern, Caribbean, and Japanese, in addition to exploring American idioms like R&B, funk, rock, and disco.

My research into Herbie's life could not have been completed without the help of his third wife, Janeal. Despite battling cancer herself, she and her husband, Aaron, were generous not only in answering all the questions that I did not get to ask Herbie, but also in lending me items from Herbie's scrapbooks for study and for use as illustrations. Nobody could be more kind, gracious, generous, and encouraging about my work than she has been.

In addition, Herbie's sister Judi Solomon Kennedy was of invaluable help in detailing Herbie's early life, heretofore undocumented. Herbie's eldest daughter, Claudia, also contributed cogent and frank observations of her father's private life and his first two marriages. I am also indebted to Marty Ashby and the Manchester Craftsmen's Guild for providing access to photographs and recordings from Herbie's personal archive, donated after his death.

I'd also like to thank John Cerullo and Marybeth Keating of Hal Leonard Books for acceding to my decision that Herbie Mann's story be told as part of their Jazz Biography Series. In addition, the following individuals and organizations provided me with other resources that proved helpful in my research: Anthony Barnett, Eddy Determeyer, Sherwin Dunner, Mike Fitzgerald, Ira Gitler, Renee Govanucci, Dr. Monika Herzig of Indiana University, Cindy Jo Hinkleman, Steven Lasker, Bill Majetic, Geoff Mann, Howard Mandel, Joan Merrill, Dan Morgenstern, Marcello Piras, Bob Porter, Michel Ruppli, Debbie Lowe Smith, Carol Sudhalter, Neil Tesser, Bert Vuijsje, Arthur Zimmerman, the Felix E. Grant Jazz Archives, and Cullen Strawn and the Musical Instrument Museum in Phoenix, Arizona.

Finally, I'd like to express my thanks and love to my wife, Gail, for answering pointed grammatical questions and for listening to an endless playlist of Herbie Mann records for the past year and a half.

1

HERBIE'S AT THE PARAMOUNT

During his long career, Herbie Mann recorded music from all around the world, yet it wasn't until the end of his life that he decided to explore his own musical roots. A secular Jew from Eastern Europe, Herbie grew up with a burning curiosity about all musical cultures except his own. But his family's heritage points to a story commonplace among Americans in the beginning of the twentieth century: an escape from repression to an enchanting new world with promises of religious and cultural freedom.

Herbie's maternal grandfather, Samuel Brecher, was born on May 15, 1880. He married Dina Zwecker, born in 1875, while residing in Bukovina, an area whose borders are chiefly east of the Carpathian Mountains in what was then known as Austria-Hungary. The Brechers had three daughters, Pauline, Shirley, and Ruth; the last would become Herbie's mother. She was born on July 4, 1905, in the village of Illawce in Austria, an area that was part of Romania during World War I but is now part of Ukraine.

In 1910, Samuel Brecher, a rabbi, arrived in the U.S. and settled on the Lower East Side of Manhattan. By 1912, he had earned enough money that the rest of the family could join him, and on September 22 of that year, Dina and the three girls arrived at Ellis Island on the SS *Campanello*. Eventually, they moved to Brooklyn, where Samuel opened up a storefront temple on Kings Highway. When she was interviewed at age ninety-eight, Ruth recalled only being able to speak German and a little Yiddish when she arrived.

It's uncertain what Herbie's family's name was on his father's side, but Herbie's sister Judi heard it as either Todelsky, Bodetsky, Podelsky, or Podetsky. ("Podelsky" is the most likely spelling, since one branch of the family shortened it to Podell.)

Born in Russia in 1875, Herbie's paternal grandfather, Barnet Solomon, arrived at Ellis Island with his family in 1876. His grandmother Ida followed in 1898. The two met in New York and married around 1900, and, like many immigrants, Barnet went into the garment industry. In the 1910 census he is listed as a designer of ladies' dresses. The couple had three children: two daughters, Rose and Frances, and a son, Harry, born on May 30, 1902. Harry Solomon would become Herbie Mann's father. After Ida Solomon died in 1921, Barnet remarried a woman named Sarah the following year and had another son named Seymour in 1926.

Harry Solomon made his living as a furrier, a middleman between breeders and manufacturers, dealing mostly in mink, sable, and ermine. Herbie's parents were introduced at a dance by Harry's cousin Harry Lester. Harry Solomon was a sickly child, and Ruth's parents worried that he might have consumption and were initially against her marrying him because he was so thin. Consequently, the couple eloped on December 17, 1925. Eventually, Ruth's parents relented after he put on some weight, and Harry and Ruth had a proper family wedding on September 18, 1926.

As Harry become more prosperous, the couple moved to Brooklyn, where they lived on either Seventeenth or Eighteenth avenue. Eventually, they moved to Brighton Third Street in the Brighton Beach section of Brooklyn. Their first child, Herbert Jay Solomon, was born on April 16, 1930, at a hospital on Fifteenth Avenue in Borough Park.

Before going into the fur business, Herbie's father worked in vaudeville as a show boy and always loved dancing with Herbie's mother. Herbie recalled that while he was growing up, music was always playing in the house. His younger sister Judi, who was born in 1937, recalled:

> Herbie always had rhythm. We had all kinds of records in the house. Growing up with Herbie, I was the kid and he was the teenager. There was jazz, bebop, classical, and he introduced me to everything.

Herbie Mann remembered the origins of his love for music:

> I knew I loved music when I was six years old. Once I decided, that's all I ever wanted to do. My mother always had music on, not necessarily jazz, and I would play pots and pans on the windowsill. I originally wanted to be a drummer. But my cousin convinced my mother that she should take me to hear Benny Goodman, because the clarinet, for a beginner, doesn't bother the neighbors as much as the drums do. So she took me to the Paramount in 1939 at a matinee on a Saturday afternoon. I can't really say now whether it was the music or it was the power he had over the audience that attracted me. It might have been a combination of both. In any event, I got goose bumps. Benny Goodman in 1939 at the Paramount was like the Beatles. There was that kind of hysteria. So that was it. Two weeks later I had a clarinet.

The Paramount Theatre, in Times Square at 43rd Street and Broadway, was a magnificent movie palace built in 1926 that could seat 3,664. (Today, it is an office building that has retained landmark status.) Its ten-story-high sign on the building's facade promoted the biggest stars of the day, including Bing Crosby, Rudy Vallée, Fred Waring, and all of the top swing orchestras of the big band era, including those of Tommy Dorsey, Harry James, and Glenn Miller, in addition to hosting frequent appearances by the Goodman orchestra. Herbie's sister Judi recalled:

> When I was old enough to notice, my question to my mother was always, "Where's Herbie?" And she'd say, "Herbie's at the Paramount." He went there whenever he could go. It was a great time to live, with all the stage shows. We heard Benny Goodman, Woody Herman, all this wonderful music coming for the price of a ticket, which cost maybe a buck. He probably cut school half the time to do it. He wanted to be like Benny Goodman and to have the ability to play with a symphony orchestra.

Herbie's third wife, Janeal, put it more succinctly when she said, "He really wanted to be admired and to be famous. He watched the people respond to Benny Goodman and how they clamored over him and adored him, and Herbie really wanted that. He was unabashed about it."

In 1940, the family moved a few blocks north to a first-floor corner apartment at 2134 Homecrest at Avenue U in the Sheepshead Bay section of Brooklyn. With music constantly spinning in his head, Herbie was not a great student at P.S. 153, Cunningham Junior High, or Abraham Lincoln High School. His sister remembered him as a "dreamer," always looking out the school window and thinking about someday becoming a famous musician. He never saw any reason to study history when there was so much music to listen to outside that window.

By the time he was fifteen or sixteen, Herbie was already playing jobs around Brooklyn and even at hotels in the Catskill Mountains. "Not jazz jobs," Herbie recalled. "Weddings, bar mitzvahs, clubs. I played gigs, I played the tenor sax, I played the flute, I played Latin music, and even a little klezmer on the clarinet. But not very much."

In addition to music, Herbie liked drawing and was a talented cartoonist (Disney characters were his favorites to draw), although none of his drawings survive. His father tried to get him involved in the fur trade, but Herbie showed no interest. When he was fourteen, he started a business called Blue-Jay Stamp Service, buying and reselling postage stamps. He also enjoyed photography and started a darkroom in his bathroom.

He developed a keen sense of style and fashion almost from the very beginning. At one time, he worked as a stock boy at a men's store around the corner from his home. "He dressed all his wives," Judi Solomon Kennedy recalled. "He was always a fashion plate."

Herbie Solomon graduated from Abraham Lincoln High School in 1948. Bearing no real affection for his high school years, he had no interest in keeping his class ring and gave it to his sister instead. He never had a lot of friends in high school. His best friends, Freddie Goldstein and Norman Perlmutter, lived down the block, but he was still basically a loner and an introvert, a nearsighted, shy Jewish boy who wore thick, horn-rimmed glasses. He played clarinet in the high school band, but by his senior year had changed his musical allegiance from Goodman to Coleman Hawkins. Herbie recalled:

My whole high school career was very frustrating. There was a clique of musicians who put me down and wouldn't let me play because they started listening earlier than I did. They were already listening to Diz [Dizzy Gillespie] and Prez [Lester Young], and I was listening to Hawk.

After Hawkins, Herbie's next idol was saxophonist Illinois Jacquet, before he finally settled on Lester Young. Herbie switched from clarinet to tenor sax and started listening to bebop, dreaming of being the next tenor sax sensation. His music teacher suggested he take lessons on the flute as well, since most studio musicians who played reed instruments were required to play all woodwinds. "I never thought of the flute as a jazz instrument," Herbie later said. "There was no reason to. In 1943, 1944, and 1945, there were no jazz flute records."

But after graduating from high school in 1948, Herbie discovered a flute record that changed his entire outlook on music and became the benchmark for his entire musical philosophy.

2

JUNGLE FANTASY

The flute has a long history in virtually every culture in the world. Some of the oldest existing instruments from antiquity are "aerophones," defined as any instrument that produces sound by causing a stream of air to vibrate. Flutelike instruments have been unearthed from civilizations that thrived some fifty thousand years ago. Today, the flute has a major role in virtually all folk and classical traditions, but its integration into jazz is relatively recent. Viewed as a timid, feminine-sounding instrument in a field dominated by male musicians, the flute was mainly used as a doubling instrument for saxophonists. In the days before microphones were introduced in the 1920s, flutes were difficult to capture on record. Although flute solos existed on jazz records before World War II, they were few and far between, and solos never lasted for more than eight or twelve bars at a time.

The earliest known appearance of an improvised flute solo on a jazz or dance band record is an eight-bar, twelve-second-long solo by an anonymous musician on "Song of the Wanderer," an otherwise banal dance band record made by Duke Yellman's Parody Club Pals, recorded for Edison on December 24, 1926.

Jazz flute solos such as the one on the Yellman disc popped up occasionally during the 1930s and '40s, played by such reed specialists as Wayman Carver and Walter "Foots" Thomas, but it was a Cuban musician named Alberto Socarrás who became the most influential of the early jazz flutists. Born in 1908, Socarrás was a classically trained musician who immigrated to the U.S. to escape the repressive racism against blacks in Cuba. He learned to play saxophone by listening to Rudy Wiedoeft records and eventually picked up the flute as well as clarinet. Upon arriving in New York, Socarrás worked in Harlem dance and theater orchestras, where he met bandleader Clarence Williams. During the next four years, Socarrás recorded flute on eight Williams 78s, the earliest a twelve-bar solo on Williams's recording of "Shooting the Pistol," waxed for Paramount in July 1927.

In the early 1930s, Socarrás was a featured soloist in Lew Leslie's *Blackbirds Revue of 1933.* In 1934 he formed a group that played Latin-tinged jazz in Harlem nightspots such as the Cotton Club and Small's Paradise. He also led the house band at the new Club Cubanacan, which broadcast live remotes on WMCA New York. Socarrás became Cuba's answer to Duke Ellington, engaging in battles-of-the-bands with the orchestras of Fletcher Henderson, Luis Russell, and Willie Bryant. In 1935 he recorded for Columbia/Brunswick, resulting in one of the first examples of fusing Cuban music and jazz.

In 1937, Socarrás made records with a New York rumba band called Antobal's Cubans, but soon left Harlem to manage Anacoana, an all-girl dance band from Havana. He returned to the U.S. in 1939 to form another orchestra, hiring a dynamic young trumpet player named Dizzy Gillespie. Gillespie later credited Socarrás with influencing him to add Latin percussion instruments into his band, which helped bring Afro-Cuban music into jazz.

In 1947, Socarrás cut the first of several sessions for RCA Victor, the records issued in the label's Latin American series as by "Socarrás and his Magic Flute." These recordings constitute the first full-length jazz flute records, as Socarrás melded his scintillating style into a series of mesmerizing rumbas and mambos.

Herbie Mann was not aware of Socarrás when he was growing up, and although he did become familiar with him in the 1950s, he didn't have access to Socarrás's RCA Victor records, which were most likely distributed only in the Cuban areas of Manhattan. It was another immigrant flutist named Esy Morales who made a record that had a lasting influence on Herbie's career.

Born in Puerto Rico in 1916, Esy Morales was the younger brother of mambo king Noro Morales, a pianist who recorded prolifically for a number of record labels during the 1940s. (For a time after he arrived from Puerto Rico in 1935, Noro Morales played in Alberto Socarrás's orchestra.) Along with their brother Humberto, the Moraleses started their own rumba orchestra in 1939, but Noro's biggest fame came after he reduced his group to a sextet and started playing Latin nightclubs in the New York City area. Unlike the classically trained Socarrás, Esy Morales was an instinctive musical genius and a master technician on the flute. He developed a virile, exotic style that dispelled any notions of the flute being a lightweight, feminine-sounding instrument. Esy's style was totally unlike that of Socarrás. He played with wild abandon, his solos laced with acrobatic, multi-octave swoops, whiplike articulation, and unworldly, exotic-sounding flutter tonguing. After leaving his brother's orchestra, Morales became a featured performer with Cuban bandleader Xavier Cugat, but then decided to start his own group.

Described as "The World's Most Unique Flutist," Morales made his first record under his own name for the New York--based Rainbow label in late 1947. The "A" side of the record, an atmospheric Afro-Cuban number called "Jungle Fantasy," became so popular in the New York area that Morales and his band were hired to appear in the 1949 Universal Pictures film noir *Criss Cross*, starring Burt Lancaster. In a nightclub scene at the beginning of the film, Morales, resplendent in a white tuxedo, plays "Jungle Fantasy" while Lancaster's character jealously eyes sultry Yvonne DeCarlo, as she dances with a handsome young extra (Tony Curtis, making his first film appearance).

After *Criss Cross*, Morales recorded more sides for other labels, including Manor and Decca, on which his fiery solos virtually flew off of the grooves. Morales's flute playing went hand in hand with the arrival of the atomic age: incendiary, and almost as explosive. But his fame was short-lived. On November 2, 1950, he died from a sudden heart attack, brought on by excessive drug use, most likely cocaine. He was just thirty-four years old.

When Herbie Mann discovered "Jungle Fantasy," he couldn't get enough of the record. "He loved the jungle beat," his sister Judi Solomon Kennedy recalled. "He felt it. Esy did more things with the flute than anyone else ever dreamed of doing. That's why he was drawn to that record. And that's why the first stuff he did on the flute was Afro-Cuban."

Although Herbie Mann was still primarily a tenor saxophonist, he kept tinkering with the flute, trying to find ways to use the tricks he heard on "Jungle Fantasy." It would be some years before he figured out not only how to incorporate Morales's techniques into his own playing, but also realized he could improvise on the flute in styles besides Afro-Cuban music. It was a long and slow process, but as he gained experience in the 1950s as a successful studio musician specializing in bebop, Herbie kept revisiting "Jungle Fantasy," especially when a song called for a more exotic approach. The record had a huge impact in shaping his style and his embrace of world music. In interviews, he always credited "Jungle Fantasy" with jump-starting his career as a jazz flutist, and recorded the song on multiple occasions throughout his career, as well as performing it in concert appearances.

3

TRIESTE

Although "Jungle Fantasy" helped Herbie Mann understand how the flute could be used as a jazz instrument, it wasn't his first introduction to Afro-Cuban music. As he explained in 1995:

> When I heard Norman Granz combine the Machito band with Dizzy, Charlie Parker, Flip Phillips, and those people, it dawned on me that what was natural for Latin music, which was improvising, could also be done on a different level with jazz players playing with Latin rhythms. That was in the mid-forties. I didn't think about being a jazz flutist until 1951. When I played the flute in the late forties, I only thought of it as an instrument to play mambos and cha-chas. I never thought of it as a jazz instrument. Even though Wayman Carver played it in the Chick Webb band and Harry Klee played it out in California, I think there was still that real limited mental concept of thinking that it's too feminine an instrument, whatever that means, and it has to be masculine to be jazz, whatever *that* means. I think what it took is for someone with enough chutzpah to say, "Well, I don't care what anybody else thinks, I'm going to go do this."

But by the time Herbie graduated from high school, he was still not thinking about using the flute in ways other than playing Latin-style novelty songs. He still had his sights set on being a tenor saxophonist in the Woody Herman orchestra. To him, that was the ultimate role he could play in music.

When Herbie turned eighteen, he registered for the draft, but because of his 20/200 eyesight, he was categorized as 4-F. "He was blind as a bat without his glasses," his sister Judi recalled. Although he played the occasional gig on tenor sax, he still had no idea what he would do with his life.

In June 1950, the United States began sending troops to Korea and Herbie's draft admission was reassessed. Rather than get drafted and sent to Korea like his friend Norman Perlmutter, he went to Governors Island, auditioned for the Army, and was accepted. He was assigned to serve in the 98th Army Band in Trieste, a seaport on the northeastern coast of Italy, bordering what was then Yugoslavia. His base of operations was the Miramare Castle, a stone structure built in the mid-nineteenth century on a promontory point at Grignano, overlooking the Gulf of Trieste in the northeastern corner of the Adriatic Sea. The castle served as headquarters for the American garrison TRUST (Trieste United States Troops) from 1947 to 1954. The picturesque grounds included an extensive cliff and seashore park originally designed by Austrian Archduke Ferdinand Maximilian.

Joining Herbie in the 98th Army Band was Don Preston, whose father was a trumpet player in the Tommy Dorsey orchestra. Preston played piano, but when he got to Trieste, switched to string bass. Aside from their regular duties playing in the marching band, musicians of the 98th often broke into smaller combos and jammed on bebop tunes. It was in one of these groups that Preston met Herbie, whom he recalled as very helpful to him in learning song structure. In later years, Preston became the original keyboardist with Frank Zappa's Mothers of Invention, from the band's inception in the 1960s until 1974. Preston's roommate in the 98th was trumpet player Buzz Gardner, also an early Zappa musician.

In addition to playing with other American musicians, Herbie jammed with local Italian bands. The Italian musicians idolized American bebop players and did their utmost to copy their styles, much to the amusement of the Americans. Drummer Sergio Conti recalled:

> There was a fantastic period in many clubs where we could play only jazz, especially in 1950 when Herbie Mann came. He was

playing tenor saxophone in the Army band, but often came and played flute with us. In the evening he left the Miramare Castle where his place was located and joined us in the clubs.

One of the bands Herbie is known to have played with was an octet led by local pianist Franco Russo, which performed at a club for American customers called the Wagon Wheel, in addition to playing three times a week on Radio Trieste. Herbie played mostly tenor sax in the 98th Army Band, which was led until 1951 by Hugh Frost, but had his flute with him for when the jazz combos in town wanted to play mambos. Herbie and the other musicians in the small combos got invaluable experience playing with the local players at various jobs around Trieste. Through musicians like Buzz Gardner, Herbie became exposed to a wide range of other kinds of music, especially avant-garde classical composers like Arnold Schoenberg, Alban Berg, and Anton Webern. But more importantly for his future work as a studio musician, he was reintroduced to more melodic composers like Ravel and Debussy, whose works he was already familiar with from records in the Solomon household.

During his time in Trieste, Herbie compiled a scrapbook of his various activities with his unit. It was more like a country club vacation than a stint in the Army. With his buddies, Herbie attempted skiing at the Cortina ski resort, played on the company basketball team (his nickname was "Bop" Solomon), played piccolo in the Army concert band, and in May 1951, enjoyed a half-day auto tour of Paris. His third wife, Janeal, recalled:

Going to Trieste was a huge thing for him. It was a tremendously transforming time, I think, that opened his eyes in a way that really helped him see larger horizons than he could ever have imagined before. He would always talk about Trieste as being a turning point in his life.

In July 1952, Herbie was discharged and returned home to Brooklyn. His sister Judi was delighted to have him back.

He hadn't changed physically but I noticed that he was a lot more worldly. I remember that he had now decided that all the food my grandmother made that he turned his nose up now tasted delicious. He was more sophisticated and had more of an idea what he wanted to do. He wanted to play music for a living. So he started looking for work. He joined the union and looked for any place to play that he could. But it was still just clarinet and saxophone. I remember him once talking about playing drums at a dance for the deaf. The drummer had the hardest job of all because the dancers had to be able to feel the beat through their feet, since they couldn't hear. Although he didn't get any regular gigs, Herbie made some good friends along the way.

Shortly after arriving home from Trieste, Herbie enrolled in the Manhattan School of Music, near Columbia University in the Morningside Heights area of New York City. Herbie was one of many jazz greats who got musical training at the conservatory. Others included Max Roach, Donald Byrd, Herbie Hancock, John Lewis, Johnny Mandel, Phil Woods, and two musicians who later became proficient on jazz flute: Yusef Lateef and Paul Horn. Herbie stayed with the college until he graduated in 1954. Phil Woods studied at the Manhattan School in 1949 before transferring to Juilliard, but remembered playing with Herbie at one of Phil's early club dates.

It was at Tony's Bar and Grill on Flatbush Avenue. Back in those days, there were a million joints like that in all the boroughs. It was an easier time for musicians because there were lots of gigs. It was on-the-job training. Everybody was on the same page, learning the Great American Songbook, Gershwin, Cole Porter, and stuff like that. At Tony's we used to play jam sessions, and if you played at least one song, Tony would give you a bowl of spaghetti—and we were all hungry in those days. So Herbie would come in and play a tune and get a glass of wine and a bowl of spaghetti. He had just gotten out of the Army and was still Herbie Solomon. He also used to come play at a joint I played in Brighton Beach, Brooklyn, called the Pink Elephant. Tony's was the place I first saw him play, but I used to see him more at the Pink Elephant after that. Bill Evans told me once that he went to the Pink Elephant, too, but was too shy to play. One thing about Herbie: he was never shy about playing.

Woods also recalled that Herbie's talents for jazz were still in the developmental stages:

> He wasn't too sharp with his improvising in those days. In Tony's Bar, where I first heard him play, we were playing "Perdido" and he asked me where the bridge should go. It's a basic "I Got Rhythm" bridge, but we never told him. [*Laughs*] He was a Lester Young fan, but Al Cohn was his big hero back then. Lester Young by way of Al Cohn was a nice way to go. He had the right ingredients.
>
> Herbie was always a hustler. He was bold as brass, but in a nice way. He was playing tenor sax in those days. We used to hang out at Charlie's Tavern and on union days, which were Monday, Wednesday, and Friday. There was a whole gang of us guys from Brighton Beach, and he was just one of the guys.

It was after he joined the musicians' union that Herbie decided to change his professional name. It was something expected in those days, especially for anyone with an ethnic-sounding name. His sister Judi recalled, "He changed his name from Solomon to Mann as soon as he got his first job. Everybody changed their names back then. Nobody was Italian; nobody was Jewish. You had to sound American. You'd find a stage name that people could remember and could roll off the tongue. 'Herbie Mann' was an 'aka.' Anytime he signed anything, he was still Herbert Solomon. So he never changed his name officially." When asked about the name change, Herbie downplayed it by saying, with a characteristic wink, "It just had a better rhythmic sound to it. Herbie Mann. Dah-dah-DUM."

4

INVENTING A STYLE

At the end of 1952, while playing in a Brooklyn nightclub, a chance encounter with a band playing in a neighboring club resulted in a change in direction for the twenty-two-year-old Herbie Mann. It was at this club where he met accordionist Mat Mathews.

Born Mathieu Herbert Wijnandts Schwarts in the Hague, Netherlands, in June 1924, Mathews took up music during World War II mainly to stay out of the hands of the Nazis after his country was invaded. "Every boy from eighteen to twenty-five was supposed to become a superman and go to work in the factories," Mathews later told *DownBeat*, "but in the early stages of the occupation, people in the so-called 'cultural' professions were excused."

Incarcerated in a concentration camp, Mathews escaped with the help of the underground resistance, which supplied him with false identification papers and a pseudonym while traveling on a Nazi train bound for Germany. During the last three months of the war, he hid in the attic of his mother's house, terrified as the Nazis made daily raids.

After the war, Mathews heard a radio broadcast on the Armed Forces Network featuring a band led by blind American accordionist Joe Mooney. This convinced him to start his own quartet, which he led for a year in Luxembourg. He hated the ricky-ticky sound associated with the accordion, so he decided to develop a different sound for the instrument.

In Germany, Mathews met an actress named Paulette Girard, who was touring with Special Services. Girard eventually joined Mathews as a singer, and in July 1951, the two were married in Tripoli, North Africa, and waited for Mathews's immigration papers to go through. After arriving in New York on March 1, 1952, Mathews signed up with the New York musician's union, Americanized his name, and started waiting the required six months before he could perform professionally. In the meanwhile, he experimented with a five-row button accordion he had bought, while a friend crafted a special microphone/amplifier setup for him.

Mat Mathews was a huge bebop fan, and was especially fond of the swinging piano/vibraphone sound of British pianist George Shearing's quintet. The Shearing style was marked by complex harmonies that blended swing, bop, and classical influences. In late 1952, Mathews decided to develop his own version of the piano/vibes sound. Herbie recalled:

A friend of mine was a drummer who was working in a club on Flatbush Avenue in Brooklyn. Right next door was another club. And my friend said, "You know, there's a guy in this other club—his name is Mat Mathews—he's making a record with the intermission singer, whose name is Carmen McRae. He's using Percy Heath on bass and Kenny Clarke on drums. Do you know if there's anybody who plays jazz on flute?" At that time, my flute experience was still Esy Morales and "Jungle Fantasy." When I went into the Army, I wanted to be Lester Young. That's all I thought of. When I got out, I found out that Stan Getz, Al Cohn, Zoot Sims, Brew Moore, and Allen Eager had beaten me to it. But I still only thought I was going to be a jazz tenor player.

Mat had the idea to take the concept of George Shearing, which was piano, vibes, and guitar in locked harmonies, and substitute the piano for accordion and the vibes for flute. So my friend asked me if I played jazz on flute. "I haven't until now," I said, "but let me take a shot at it." The only one in New York who was known to play jazz on flute was Sam Most. So my friend called Mat and said, "Sam's out of town, but I know somebody who I think could do it." So I met with Mat and told him that my flute was being repaired, which was a lie. That weekend I listened to the one jazz flute record there was: Sam Most playing "Undercurrent Blues." It gave me kind of an idea on how to go about it. Sam had a very distinctive style that was kind of like his clarinet playing. But there was no style for flutists playing jazz. You couldn't listen to the Charlie Parker or the Lester Young or the Dizzy Gillespie of flute playing. So I said to myself, "Why not listen to trumpet players?" So I listened to Miles and Dizzy and Art Farmer and Clifford Brown, and that's what I based my style on. It was more percussive. It wasn't like the prevailing notion of the flute. Nobody plays jazz on the saxophone like classical saxophone, and nobody plays jazz on the bass like classical bass. The same goes for piano and trumpet. So I said, "I can't base it on William Kincaid, so I'm just going to develop my own style.

The music that Mat was playing was bebop. Kenny Clarke was a helluva drummer. He played great brushes. The problem with me later on is that my first rhythm section was Kenny Clarke and Percy Heath. You can get spoiled very easily."

Herbie's first recording session took place early in 1953, probably in January, for Jubilee, a New York-based label that specialized in pop and doo-wop. It is likely that four songs were recorded, the usual number at union sessions, but only two have been documented: a jazz version of "Elegie" by Jules Massenet, and "Poor Butterfly," a pop song inspired by Puccini's opera *Madame Butterfly*. The two titles were issued on Jubilee 6035 and most likely sold only in the New York City area. In an October 1953 profile in *DownBeat* magazine, Mathews optimistically recalled that the Jubilee sides were "mildly successful," but copies are extremely scarce and most discographies still show empty data for that record number. Herbie himself confirmed that he had recorded with Mathews for Jubilee, but revealed no details about the session.

Herbie's next session with the Mathews quintet was made for the Stardust label; they backed singer Carmen McRae on two songs, "Wanting You" and "A Foggy Day," released as Stardust 1002. In *DownBeat*, Mathews recalled recording a series of demos with his quintet and McRae and then shopping them around town to see if anyone was interested. On the Stardust session, Percy Heath was replaced on bass by Wendell Marshall, while McRae's then-husband, Kenny Clarke, played drums. The fifth member of Mathews's group was twenty-year-old guitarist Mundell Lowe, who recalled:

Mat hired me because I had worked with Carmen McRae before. She suggested he call me, which he did, and I guess that's when Herbie first showed up. I started with Carmen when she used to play at Minton's Playhouse up in Harlem, where she was playing solo piano and singing. This would have been in the late forties or 1950. The first records she made, which kind of put her in business, were with Mat Mathews. The Stardust records were made across the street from Carnegie Hall in a little studio upstairs. She also put in some requests for sidemen. Carmen played piano and was very picky who she worked with. She and Mat seemed to have a good musical relationship, so they agreed who should be on the session. I knew nothing about Herbie until I met him when he suddenly showed up for this date. I had never even heard of him. After that, he became a studio musician and I used to use him on some of my dates.

The "little studio upstairs" that Lowe is referring to is probably the Penthouse Sound Studios at 113 West 57th Street, run by Vincent J. Nola, whose son Tommy was the engineer. Nola hosted many jazz recording sessions during that period, including those by Ella Fitzgerald and guitarist Chuck Wayne, among others.

The same group that made the Stardust record apparently made another one, at an unknown date, probably shortly afterward in 1953, with two sides released on the Venus label: "Old Devil Moon," from *Finian's Rainbow*, and an original song written by Mathews and his wife Paulette Girard called "Tip Toe Gently." According to Lowe, the recordings were owned by McRae and later sold to Bethlehem Records, where they were reissued as part of her first Bethlehem album. (The two Stardust sides were released on an LP along with six other early McRae sides, on which she was backed by the orchestras of Larry Elgart and Sy Oliver.) Herbie stayed in the background on these initial sides, limited to playing ethereally in the background, but he did contribute a sultry, Stan Getz--influenced solo on the swinging "Tip Toe Gently." Two other songs were recorded at the session: Cole Porter's "Easy to Love" and "If I'm Lucky," the latter a new song composed by Girard, with lyrics by Chuck Darwin.

The four McRae sides were issued in 1954 on one side of McRae's eponymous ten-inch LP debut on Bethlehem, along with four other sides she made with Tony Scott's quartet later in the year. *DownBeat* praised McRae's singing, but called the two songs contributed by Girard "weak," while the recording of "Old Devil Moon" was termed "lifeless." (Bethlehem took *DownBeat*'s critique to heart. When stereo recording came in, they overdubbed an electric guitar, vibraphone, and echo onto "Old Devil Moon.")

On April 29, 1953, the Mat Mathews Quintet recorded a full session for Brunswick Records, consisting of nine standards and three Mathews originals. Guitarist Benny Weeks replaced Mundell Lowe, while Percy Heath returned to play bass. In July, the first single from the Brunswick session got the Mathews quintet its first review in *DownBeat*. "Owl Eyes," written by Mathews and Girard—which became the theme song for WNEW disc jockey Al "Jazzbo" Collins's radio program—was a slow, thoughtful tune that reviewer Nat Hentoff praised for its charming chord changes and Herbie's "fluent flute." The flip side, the Rodgers and Hart classic "There's a Small Hotel," got a faster workout, displaying "good time and good taste," as described by Hentoff.

In August, the Mathews band was offered an off-night gig at Birdland, the famous midtown jazz club named for Charlie "Bird" Parker. The response was positive enough to warrant the group being booked for two weeklong engagements. Herbie had been living at home with his parents in Brooklyn, but after work picked up with the Mathews band, he rented an apartment in Greenwich Village.

A second single, issued in October, paired the Johnny Mercer/David Raksin standard "Laura" with "Study in Purple," an original composition by Mathews. "Laura" featured only Mathews's accordion with bass and drums, but Herbie was praised for his tenor playing on the minor-key "Study in Purple." Reviewer Nat Hentoff predicted "a big future" for the quintet.

The third single from the Brunswick session appeared in December, featuring Milt Jackson's "Bag's Groove" (sic) backed with the standard "The Nearness of You." On the former song, Herbie took the lead, with Mathews harmonizing behind him, followed by solos from each. (Herbie was listed as "Herb Mann" on the Brunswick 78 and 45 rpm labels.) By now, Hentoff was becoming convinced that the flute, as played by Herbie, "could be a standard jazz instrument," but complained about the briefness of the solos. "Nearness" was snidely dismissed as "mostly for the cocktail trade and the Gabor sisters."

Song length would be a problem that plagued Herbie and other jazz musicians throughout much of the 1950s, as record companies (especially Bethlehem) insisted on releasing albums with eight songs, four on each side, the standard for ten-inch pop records. When the format expanded to twelve-inch LPs, the number of total tracks grew to twelve, but the standard three-minute length of the songs rarely varied. Jazz records slowly emerged from this tradition in the 1950s, when labels like Norman Granz's Clef (and later Verve) and Bob Weinstock's Prestige broke through by recording longer cuts, enabling musicians to stretch out in their solos.

The fourth and final single from the session, which wasn't released until June 1954, included "Maya," an atmospheric original by Mathews, backed with what was probably the best song of the session, a rip-roaring version of Cole Porter's "Night and Day." For the first time, Herbie's quickly developing technical mastery of the flute's high register was showcased, and in one particularly vivid sequence, he used double-tonguing to match the flurry of notes played by Mathews's accordion and Weeks's guitar. The combination of the flute and accordion, both instruments that had been previously alien to jazz, was being hailed as not only a fresh, but a hip addition to the usual spectrum of trumpets and saxophones.

At this session, Herbie Mann also introduced another instrument new to jazz, the alto flute, which he played on one track, the album cut "Spring It Was," which is probably the first time the alto flute was featured on a jazz record. Herbie waxed poetic about his love for the alto flute in interviews throughout his career:

> Alto flute is the most beautiful-sounding instrument I think there is. You know, when Max Roach and Art Blakey used to come to the clubs to hear me play, they'd say, "Play the big one."

By this time, Herbie Mann had established himself as a solid player on the New York studio scene. Although other musicians, like Jerome Richardson, Sam Most, and Frank Wess were also playing flute, Herbie Mann was the first to specialize on the instrument. The tenor sax was already taking a backseat to his flute playing, and before long, Herbie routinely got the first calls for a flute player on New York studio sessions. These would increase dramatically beginning in 1954. He would spend much of the next five years virtually living in the studios, cementing his reputation as the leader in a new wave of jazz innovation in the 1950s.

But behind all of this acclaim and success, Herbie was already beginning to feel boxed in by the limitations of bebop.

5

THE OWL RISES

In September 1954, Herbie Mann was hired to play flute, alto flute, and tenor sax in a twenty-piece touring band assembled by former Stan Kenton arranger Pete Rugolo. Plans for a long-playing album featuring the group were also in the works. Herbie had developed a reputation through his work with Mat Mathews at Birdland and was attracting the attention of composers and arrangers on the New York scene. Before long, he was being called frequently to do record dates when he wasn't performing with Mathews.

While playing in the Rugolo orchestra, Herbie participated in a recording session for an album designed to interpolate jazz into the annual Christmas holiday season. The project was the idea of jazz critic Leonard Feather, who often moonlighted as a composer himself, having written hits for singer Dinah Washington like "Evil Gal Blues" and playing passable jazz piano with various all-star groups.

Feather composed an eight-movement suite, with each section representing the mood and personality suggested by the reindeer in Clement Clarke Moore's 1823 poem "A Visit from St. Nicholas." The result, *Winter Sequence: A Seasonal Suite for Rhythmic Reindeer,* was arranged by Ralph Burns and issued on a ten-inch M-G-M LP in time for the 1954 Christmas season. Herbie's flying flute represented "Dasher," while the other reindeer were represented by saxophonist Danny Bank (Dancer), pianist Ralph Burns (Prancer), trombonist Kai Winding (Vixen), bassist and cellist Oscar Pettiford (Comet), guitarist Billy Bauer (Cupid), drummer

Osie Johnson (Donner) and trumpeter Joe Wilder (Blitzen). A whimsical line drawing of the group, with Feather cracking a whip over the musicians, each astride a reindeer, was featured on the album cover. A bespectacled Herbie, riding alongside Burns, led the pack.

The Rugolo orchestra featured some fine, innovative writing and arranging by its leader but couldn't hold up as a touring group and folded within two months. Before the Rugolo band broke up, it recorded the Columbia LP *Rugolomania*. Herbie was featured on three tracks (an additional tune was released on the Harmony LP *New Sounds*) and was showcased on "Everything I Have Is Yours" and the Latin-tinged "Hornorama."

The usual problem encountered by flutists in a big band is their inability to be heard over the blasting horn and saxophone sections. While playing with Rugolo's orchestra, Herbie arrived at a solution to help alleviate the problem, especially when he played the much quieter alto flute.

Pete came to New York looking for a band to form after he left Stan Kenton. And he had already made a record out on the West Coast. I don't know the reason why he came to New York. Maybe all those guys on the West Coast were studio players and were working too much. So he came to New York, and I was the only flute player in New York who owned an alto flute. So I got the job.

Pete used to write for alto flute and trombone, alto flute and French horn, and alto flute and flugelhorn. Alto flute is the perfect instrument. I always thought that the best band you could have would be alto flute, flugelhorn, cello, and acoustic guitar, and I wanted to form a band called the Warmers. That would have been perfect. The velvet of the alto flute can wrap around any instrument. It has always been my favorite.

When you're playing an instrument that's in the key of G, and everybody else is playing B-flat and E-flat instruments, you certainly learn how to play keys! Every note you're looking at is not that note. There was no lead alto saxophone. It was lead alto flute.

It was Pete's first big band, and it was also my first big band. The rest of the musicians were hardened road warriors. And I saw that he was in big trouble, so I volunteered to become the road manager to help him out.

When I was playing with Pete, I played lead alto flute over the sax section. We could never hear ourselves onstage; my microphone was going into the house. I was playing lead, and the guys were guessing as to what the lead was because the alto flute is a very low-sounding instrument and they couldn't hear me. So I said to Pete, "I've got an idea. Give me a guitar amp and a microphone and I'll set up the guitar amp behind me." So we started doing that.

Herbie's first recording session after the Rugolo orchestra broke up showed him experimenting with Afro-Cuban rhythms for the first time. The session was produced and arranged by twenty-one-year-old wunderkind Quincy Jones, featuring a quintet led by tenor saxophonist Paul Quinichette, known as "Vice Prez" because of the similarity of his sound to that of Lester Young. Quinichette's group also included piano, bass, and drums, augmented by a percussion section of conga drums, bongos, and timbales, standard-issue instruments for Herbie's sessions in the latter part of the decade. Four songs were cut on November 22, 1954, constituting half of Quinichette's EmArcy LP, *Moods*. At this session, Herbie's effervescent flute style made its first appearance. Previously, he had either played from prepared charts or supplied relatively tentative solos in line with the predilection for "lightweight" flute playing during this period. Herbie's virile solos on both flute and piccolo on the *Moods* album showed him flexing his Esy Morales muscles for the first time, especially on "Grasshopper" and "Dilemma Diablo," both Afro-Cuban-flavored Quincy Jones originals.

If Herbie had an epiphany after recording the four Afro-Cuban sides, it didn't have an immediate effect on his repertoire, as he continued playing mainly bebop flute behind small combos and jazz vocalists. The Quinichette session led to his next date in December, backing Sarah Vaughan, who was recording for Decca.

Prior to the Vaughan session, Herbie signed a three-year, seven-album deal with Bethlehem Records and made his first record with his own group. Bethlehem had recently initiated its "East Coast Jazz" series, whose first three volumes focused on compositions by Bobby Scott, recordings by the Vinnie Burke Quartet, and guitarist Joe Puma's combo. Herbie's first group featured Benny Weeks on guitar, Keith Hodgson on bass, and Lee Rockey on drums. Both Weeks and Rockey had played with Neal Hefti's first band. Weeks and Herbie had worked frequent gigs with Mat Mathews, so they felt comfortable in putting together their first album as a group.

The album, titled *East Cost Jazz Series No. 4*, was issued on a ten-inch LP. "A group that has a flute in it should be a light swinging, happy sounding one," Herbie said in the liner notes. "It must be surrounded with instruments which do not weigh it down to that point at which it loses its natural character." Despite the four Afro-Cuban numbers he had recorded with Paul Quinichette, Herbie still thought that the flute had an innately "light" sound and couldn't be featured with instruments that might overwhelm it.

After three rehearsals, the quartet was ready to record. With a young producer named Creed Taylor at the helm, they cut the session on Tuesday, December 14, 1954. Taylor was a trumpet player who was at the beginning of a long and influential career as a director and producer. The engineer was Tom Dowd, a recent hire at Atlantic Records who would become a fixture at the label in the 1960s and '70s. Herbie remembered making his first album as a leader:

> We did it at a small studio on Fortieth Street between Fifth and Sixth avenues. When you make your first record, you're thrilled about every part of it. You'll notice that "My Little Suede Shoes" was the only song that had a Latin flavor. I went through five years before I actually got into what is now known as world music. Truthfully, I found the rhythms more exciting.

Four of the six songs were Herbie's first original compositions. "After Work" reflected his daily routine of riding the subway and walking to his Village apartment, backed by a methodical, walking bass rhythm. "A Spring Morning" was more sprightly and optimistic; Herbie wrote it just before the session, thinking of sunnier weather in the spring. The swinging "Chicken Little" showcased Herbie's growing sophistication as an inventive jazz soloist.

The fourth composition, "The Purple Grotto," was written at the request of disc jockey Al "Jazzbo" Collins, who wanted Herbie to write something "moody and funky." The song was named for the fantasy subterranean lair where Collins hosted his jazz radio program on WNEW. Collins populated his world with hip creatures like Jukes, a purple chameleon, and Harrison, a Tasmanian owl, which became Collins's alter ego. (Herbie had recorded "Owl Eyes," Collins's theme song, for Mat Mathews in 1953.)

Burt Goldblatt's cover photograph showed Herbie wearing a checkered shirt with the sleeves rolled up, an owl perched on the end of his flute, staring morosely at the camera. To enhance the mysterious atmosphere of Collins's enchanted bopster world, engineer Dowd added an echo effect, which was exaggerated on one of Herbie's high-register rips on the flute, creating a virtual sonic waterfall of sound. Collins loved the effect so much he played the riff on his show whenever he mentioned the name "Purple Grotto."

By now, Collins was Herbie's most ardent supporter, promoting his local appearances in New York nightclubs and playing his records on his program whenever possible. A grateful Herbie not only allowed Collins to attend the session, but invited him to play bongos on a Latin-tinged arrangement of Charlie Parker's "My Little Suede Shoes."

Topping off the album were two standards, "Between the Devil and the Deep Blue Sea" and the contemplative "The Things We Did Last Summer," on which Herbie played alto flute. Nat Hentoff's review in *DownBeat* gave Herbie's first album an enthusiastic four stars, calling his compositions "humorous" and "unpretentious." Hentoff concluded his review by saying, "I can think of very few albums, incidentally, that would serve as well as this to introduce a newcomer to jazz."

During the remaining years of his contract with Bethlehem, Herbie Mann became a familiar face in New York recording studios, backing female vocalists and sitting in a variety of groups on flute and tenor sax. He was becoming a well-known and respected musician, but more important, slowly but surely, the flute was beginning its ascension to the ranks of standard jazz instruments.

6

MANN IS THE MOST!

Two days after his first session as a bandleader for Bethlehem, Herbie Mann was back in the studio as a sideman, as part of a sextet backing Sarah Vaughan on nine songs that would result in her eponymous debut album for EmArcy Records. Paul Quinichette, who played tenor sax, likely referred him for this session. Joining them was one of Herbie's idols, trumpeter Clifford Brown, plus pianist Jimmy Jones, bassist Joe Benjamin, and drummer Roy Haynes.

As 1955 began, Herbie continued his session work, playing with an all-star seventeen-piece orchestra led by Quincy Jones for a large-scale version of Quinichette's "Grasshopper." In April, pianist Ralph Sharon used Herbie on flute and tenor sax in a session by Bethlehem thrush Chris Connor. In years to come, Herbie appeared opposite Connor on many occasions. Her manager, Monte Kay, eventually manage Herbie as well, and Kay booked them both at New York's Village Gate, where Herbie had his first crossover success in 1961.

In June, Herbie cut his second session for Bethlehem. Again, he used the quartet configuration of flute, guitar, bass, and drums, but this time with different musicians: Joe Puma on guitar, Charles Andrus on bass, and Harold Granowsky on drums, which resulted in Herbie's first twelve-inch LP, *Flamingo* (sometimes called *Herbie Mann, Vol. 2*). Burt Goldblatt's whimsical cover artwork showed Herbie's flute played by a bright red flamingo, "fingering" the flute with one of its feet. In the liner notes, the bird's name is revealed to be Jay (Herbie's middle name), first cousin of

Harrison the Owl. On the opposite end of the flute, where the owl was perched on Herbie's first album, sat a miniature, crouching Herbie, flute in hand, mimicking the stance of the taciturn owl.

For the liner notes, Bethlehem relied on Herbie's own observations rather than employing the usual array of jazz disc jockeys, producers, and critics. A producer's note tells how the new Herbie Mann Quartet was formed that April and that Herbie was now studying flute with Fred Wilkins, a much-admired flutist with the Radio City Music Hall Orchestra who also played with the New York City Ballet and the New York City Opera. Wilkins had just been elected president of the New York Flute Club after having taught at the Manhattan School of Music, where Herbie had been studying since he was discharged from the Army. In later years, Wilkins served as vice president and educational director for the Artley Flute Company. (For much of the early part of his career, Herbie favored Artley flutes.)

With *Flamingo*, Bethlehem started taking advantage of magnetic recording tape; Joe Puma's arrangement of Jerome Kern and Oscar Hammerstein's "I've Told Ev'ry Little Star" featured Herbie overdubbing three C flutes and an alto flute on the opening chorus, paralleling Woody Herman's saxophone quartet of three tenors and a baritone, which constituted his "Four Brothers" sound of the late 1940s. Quincy Jones's blues waltz "Jasmin" featured another veritable quartet of overdubbed Herbies.

Four more Mann originals were included on the album. "Sorimaó," featuring Herbie on alto flute, was inspired by the music of Brazilian composer Heitor Villa-Lobos, the first sign of Herbie's exposure to Brazilian music, something he would explore more fully in the early 1960s after the onset of bossa nova. Herbie titled "The Influential Mr. Cohn" (which he played on tenor sax) after one of his favorite saxophonist stylists, Al Cohn, a much admired, melodically inclined player, fellow Brooklynite, and a former member of Woody Herman's vaunted "Four Brothers."

It's interesting to note that by this time, Herbie thought of himself as a flutist doubling on tenor instead of a tenor player who also played flute. This minor observation, made by Herbie in his notes, marked an important landmark in the history of jazz: the first time a jazz musician promoted himself as a specialist on the flute.

DownBeat gave the album a rave review, as reviewer Nat Hentoff praised Herbie for his lyrical musicianship and assuredness, citing his innate ability to make the flute swing. Hentoff also noted Herbie's versatility in executing different musical moods, pointing out that he was "equally convincing in happy whimsy, sorrowful ballads, hopeful ballads, swingers, the Villa-Lobos-inspired 'Sorimaó,' and even a blues waltz." The success of *Flamingo* propelled Herbie into an even busier period in the studio during the second half of the year.

Herbie was being helped out in his business affairs by Ruth Shore, his agent's secretary, whom he had started dating. Herbie's sister Judi recalled, "Ruth was actually the best thing to happen to Herbie, business-wise. She was extremely savvy, had all the contacts, and she knew the business inside and out. They saw each other for about a year or a year and a half and were living together in the Village when they got married. Ruth worked more on making sure the contracts he got were right, but I think he got his gigs on his own."

Later that month, Herbie joined Mat Mathews's group for another session backing Carmen McRae, this time adding pianist Dick Katz. In the fall, he was brought in to record with Ralph Burns, who, like Pete Rugolo, was a progressive, forward-thinking arranger, having worked with the Woody Herman orchestra. Burns's 1955 Decca LP *Jazz Studio 5* included such luminaries as veteran Count Basie trumpeter Joe Newman, trombonist Billy Byers, and bassist Milt Hinton. Herbie played four instruments on the session: flute, alto flute, piccolo, and tenor sax, and was highlighted on several tracks. His rich tenor was featured on Duke Ellington's "What Am I Here For," while on "Royal Garden Blues" he played a scintillating piccolo chase chorus with Bill Barber on tuba. On Burns's Cuban-flavored "South Gonzales Street Parade," the Esy Morales influence surfaced once again, with an effervescent flute solo by Herbie ("effective as usual," Hentoff observed in *DownBeat*).

Herbie's next Bethlehem album paired him with Sam Most, who had succeeded him as flutist with the Mat Mathews Quintet. It was Most's Prestige recording of "Undercurrent Blues," recorded in January 1953 and issued on an extended-play 45, that gave Herbie his first direction as a flutist after joining Mathews in 1953. Herbie and Sam were now both recording for Bethlehem, beginning a wave of woodwind-oriented LPs on the label. Their album, titled *The Herbie Mann/Sam Most Quintet*, was released early in 1956 and became a watershed in the development of jazz flute playing.

Born in 1930, Sam Most learned clarinet from his older brother Abe, an accomplished big-band musician during the 1940s. Ten years younger than his brother, Sam first switched to saxophone, and was influenced by bebop players like Charlie Parker and Lee Konitz. After taking up the flute, he recorded an extended-play 45 rpm disc for Prestige in January 1953 that included "Undercurrent Blues," recognized as being the first bebop flute record. Most recalled making the double-flute LP for Bethlehem with Herbie:

> I had my own group that played at Birdland on Monday nights. I was playing mostly clarinet in those days, like my brother did. I did a gig with Herbie and Mat Mathews in Toronto. Carmen McRae was on it. It might have been Monte Kay, who was running Birdland, who recommended that I get together with Herbie to do a two-flute album for Bethlehem. Russ Garcia brought in some arrangements and we did it.

DownBeat thought the album was "too much of a good thing" and longed to hear another instrument besides the guitar break up the monotony of the Mann/Most combination. Advertisements for the record played up a nonexistent rivalry between the two. "Mann is the Most!" cried one faction, while "Most is the Man!" came from the other. But the mild-mannered Most and the studious-looking Herbie were anything but musically or personally combative. The styles of the two would diverge in the ensuing years. Most stayed rooted to bebop, while the ever-restless Herbie eventually began exploring world music. Looking back, Most admired Herbie's adventurous spirit, and also recognized a deficiency in Herbie's musicality with which other musicians would later concur.

> I think I was more serious about my flute playing then he was— he didn't seem to pick his notes as carefully as I did. He was more into playing commercial, and I was heavily into bebop. One time

I told Herbie, "Wow, I wish I could be as successful as you." I was working in L.A. at that time. And Herbie said, "One of us has to be the artist and one of us has to be the businessman."

7

LIGHT AND SWINGING

As 1955 drew to a close, Herbie Mann still had not varied from his belief that the flute's role in jazz was to be light and swinging. His groups were still quartets, consisting of flute, guitar, bass, and drums, when he wasn't backing a vocalist or playing occasionally with Mat Mathews.

Late in the year, Herbie backed singer Terry Morel on a Bethlehem album recorded at the Montclair Supper Club in Jackson Heights, Long Island, with Herbie joining a quartet led by pianist Ralph Sharon. Just before New Year's, he joined a group led by pianist Hank Jones for a Savoy album backing twenty-one-year-old cabaret singer Marlene VerPlanck. (VerPlanck made other albums later in her career, but was best known as the voice behind the Campbell's Soup "Mm-mm-good" commercials.)

The new year began with Herbie appearing on an ABC-Paramount album by Don Elliott in another session produced by Creed Taylor. The album, titled *A Musical Offering by the Don Elliott Sextette*, featured Elliott doubling on mellophone and vibraphone (although he is pictured on the album cover holding a French horn). Quincy Jones's clear-cut arrangements permitted Herbie to wail a little on tenor sax, as well as playing flute and alto flute on a variety of jazz standards like "Cry Me a River," "Rough Ridin'," and "Mood Indigo," but, as Jones freely admitted in the notes, the album contained merely "polite, nonchalant, pleasing music."

By now, Herbie was not only the first-call flute player in New York, he was also being heard on NBC network broadcasts in addition to his regular Monday night appearances at Birdland. Bethlehem reissued Herbie's first

LP in the new twelve-inch format, adding four newly recorded songs to the seven from the first album. (Two other songs, "You Go to My Head" and "S' Nice" were issued as a Bethlehem single.) Herbie's sound was still "light and swinging," as reviews described it, and *DownBeat* remained complimentary of his "impressive warmth, wit, and sensitivity."

During the rest of the year, Herbie continued in this mode. It was the probably the longest stretch of his career in which he did not appear to be straining at his musical bonds. He was now successful and in demand as a flutist, although he still played tenor sax when the occasion demanded, as on a February 1956 session with the Howard McGhee Orchestra. But whereas contemporaries like Sam Most, Bud Shank, Jerome Richardson, and Buddy Collette were still primarily reedmen, the flute had become Herbie's first option.

In March, he cut his last sessions for Bethlehem. One was in a big-band setting, backing singer Frances Faye, while the other was the first in a long line of musical experiments, the first album focusing entirely on the alto flute. To heighten the inherent warmth of the instrument, Herbie was backed not by his usual guitar-and-rhythm quartet, but the orchestras of Ralph Burns and Frank Hunter. (Guitarist Joe Puma and bassist Whitey Mitchell were added to the Hunter sides, while bassist Milt Hinton replaced Mitchell on the Burns sides.)

The album, titled *Love and the Weather*, was appropriately lush and romantic, bringing to fruition another of jazz musicians' attempts to emulate the successful "Charlie Parker with Strings" sound. But Herbie still had not discovered the alto flute's moodier qualities, which he would experiment with later in his career. To him, the flute and its cousin the alto were still inherently "happy"-sounding instruments. "Happy tunes sound that way whether they're done fast or slow," he said at the time. It was clear that by using the orchestral approach to jazz, Herbie was already looking for that magical crossover sound that would take him beyond the usual jazz audiences.

The only other album of note Herbie appeared on during 1956 was with the Manhattan Jazz Septette, on an LP made for Coral in June. The desultory arrangements by Manny Albam included a song called "Flute Cocktail," but the remaining numbers were the usual mix of pop and jazz standards.

Feeling restless, Herbie booked a tour of Scandinavia, and on September 8, he and Ruth were married, making the trip their honeymoon. Ruth managed his calendar and made sure the books were properly maintained. Sometime that year, Herbie started growing a small beatnik beard, which made him look like a bespectacled Mitch Miller.

Upon their arrival in Sweden in October, Herbie made good use of his time by appearing on radio shows when he wasn't jamming and performing with local jazz musicians. In Stockholm, Herbie recorded five tracks with a quartet of Swedish bop musicians led by trombonist Åke Persson. Four days later, a two-day session with another group led by trumpeter Bengt-Arne Wallin resulted in an additional five songs. The two sessions comprised the album *Mann in the Morning*, issued in the U.S. on Prestige.

By November, Herbie was in the Netherlands, where he played flute and tenor sax with Dutch pianist Pim Jacobs's quartet, a group credited to drummer Wessel Ilcken, the popular leader of Holland's bebop movement. (In July 1957, the thirty-three-year-old Ilcken died tragically of a stroke.) Once again, the mood was light and swinging, although the band was augmented on four tracks by trumpet session man Ado Broodboom, whose muted horn was his trademark.

When Herbie and Ruth returned to the U.S. three days after the Jacobs/Ilcken session, the jazz scene in midtown Manhattan showed little change. The prevailing music was still bebop, with the post-Bird atmosphere still focusing on technical bravado and endless jams on the same songs played in the same way. In 1957, however, Herbie's musical curiosity resulted in his first explorations away from bebop and the status quo in New York jazz.

8

ORGY IN RHYTHM

In 1957, Herbie Mann's Bethlehem deal was behind him and he was starting to look for new avenues to explore. He started the year by reuniting with Mat Mathews for three albums. By this time, only Herbie was doing well on the New York scene, while Mathews and his men were living from session to session. The first of the three albums was made for Elektra Records, a label established in 1951 by Jac Holzman, who would become a legendary figure after discovering Judy Collins, the Doors, and dozens of other influential artists. In the mid-fifties, Elektra was a struggling folk music label, but like Herbie, Holzman was hoping to expand his audience. Holzman's experiments with jazz didn't last long. "I was too far behind to catch up with Riverside and Bethlehem," Holzman later said. "Elektra was never going to be anybody's first choice for a jazz record. Other genres interested me more. I respected jazz, but I didn't love it enough."

Though now without a drummer, Mathews's group still included stalwarts Joe Puma on guitar and Whitey Mitchell on bass. Herbie not only played flute, but also made his initial recordings on his first instrument, the clarinet. The group, now billing itself as the New York Jazz Quintet, casually drank Cokes while working on their head arrangements in the studio. In between numbers, Herbie loosened everyone up with his impressions of Louis Armstrong and Fats Domino. "It was a two-record deal. We got along," Herbie said of Holzman. "He let us do what we wanted to do, and that's all you'd want from a record company or a producer. But at that time, jazz records didn't sell as well as records with vocalists or rock 'n' roll.

It was still Mat's record, so he was picking the tunes." The same group did another album later that month for Coral, this time calling themselves the New York Quartet. For this album, Herbie played tenor sax and got a chance to record his idol Benny Goodman's signature tune, "Don't Be That Way," on the clarinet.

The third and final album Herbie recorded with Mat Mathews, again for Elektra, was a departure from the other two. *The New York Jazz Quartet Goes Native* included two percussionists, Latin musician Manuel Ramos and Japan-born Teiji Ito, and thus had a decidedly different sound. Ito was an especially intriguing addition to the group. In 1955, he had traveled to Haiti to compose music for filmmaker Maya Deren, whom he later married. In Haiti, Ito studied ceremonial and secular drumming techniques from the Haitian master drummer known as Coyote. Mathews's idea was to combine the sounds of Latin American rhythms with jazz, something conga drum artist Chano Pozo had first done by playing with Dizzy Gillespie's orchestra in the 1940s. (More recently, guitarist Laurindo Almeida had begun exploring traditional folk music of Brazil by combining it with jazz in two landmark quartet albums for Pacific Jazz.)

The New York Jazz Quartet Goes Native marked a one-hundred-eighty-degree turn from Mathews's first Elektra effort. All but one of the songs were new compositions written by members of the band. Herbie's contributions were "March of the Sugar-Cured Hams," a Brazilian-flavored march that featured him playing piccolo lead; "Coo Coo Calypso," which he played on a handmade wooden flute he had picked up on his travels; and "The Mann Act," a jaunty tour de force featuring conga drums, bongos, and bass. The stylistic highlight of the album was a brief burst on Joe Puma's pseudo samba "Sambalu," in which Herbie's flute emulated the explosiveness of the rocket ships that were currently being shot off from Cape Canaveral. The force of this solo, with the drummers churning along behind him, showed Herbie breaking out of his bebop shell for the first time, an exhilarating, thrilling sequence that foreshadowed greater excitement to come.

Two weeks later, Herbie was brought in by drummer Art Blakey to participate in an album that not only reinforced the fusion concept of the Elektra album, but also altered Herbie's musical direction for good. Ever since getting out of the Army, Herbie had either been playing bebop with Mathews and his own small groups or backing vocalists in recording studios and nightclubs. But now he was involved in a project that opened his eyes about the possibilities the flute held for jazz.

The idea for the album was germinated in 1945, when Blue Note Records founder Alfred Lion paid a visit to Club Sudan in Upper Manhattan. Performing that night was the vaunted Billy Eckstine Orchestra, the pioneering jazz bebop band. Gene Ammons was blowing up a storm on the tenor, but Lion paid more attention to the band's drummer, Art Blakey. Blakey generated so much excitement in his performance that Lion made it a point to see him perform whenever he could. Eventually he paired Blakey with Thelonious Monk in a trio that made jazz history. Later, when Blakey formed his own band, the Jazz Messengers, he recorded a series of groundbreaking albums for Lion and Blue Note.

In 1954, Lion and Blakey decided to put together an orchestra consisting solely of drums and exotic percussion instruments. The project came to fruition three years later when the album was made, with Blakey augmenting his orchestra with a trio consisting of pianist Ray Bryant, bassist Wendell Marshall, and Herbie on flute. His percussion ensemble featured nine drummers playing a plethora of percussion instruments, including timpani, bongos, timbales, congas, maracas, *cencerro*, and even a tree log. Four jazz drummers were used: Blakey, his disciple Art Taylor, "Papa" Jo Jones from the old Count Basie orchestra, and Carmen McRae's drummer, Specs Wright. A five-man Latin rhythm section rounded out the group, consisting of Sabu, Carlos "Patato" Valdes, Jose Valiente, Ubaldo Nieto, and Evilio Quintero. (The diminutive Patato would become an integral part of Herbie's bands for the next fifteen years.) Herbie brought along his collection of hand-carved African wooden flutes and whistles he had been collecting. He played standard silver flute on only one number, "Abdallah's Delight."

On March 7, 1957, they assembled at the Manhattan Towers recording studio without the benefit of rehearsals and using no written scores. Blakey directed the band from behind his drum set while Sabu led the Latin rhythm section. Each song was performed once. To overcome the musicians' nervousness, Blakey told them, "Just listen to each other. Close your eyes and think you're home."

The very first track, "Buhaina Chant" (Buhaina was Blakey's Moslem name) opened with Jo Jones on the timpani, followed by Herbie playing a mournful melody on one of his wooden flutes. Sabu's melismatic vocal introduction was not unlike the wails of a cantor, followed by an explosion of drums led by Blakey and the Latin percussionists.

Eight songs were recorded that day, enough for two full albums of material. Most were extravaganzas for the percussionists, the trio joining in when indicated by Blakey. Although Herbie only played a supporting role at the session, hearing how his flute sounded over the percussionists was a revelation. There is little doubt that this session stimulated his concept of his flute riding on waves of percussion.

The session produced two LPs, provocatively titled *Orgy in Rhythm*—a most appropriate name, since the recordings churned with a tribal urgency that had never been heard before at a jazz recording session. The fury of the rhythms heard that day triggered a burning desire in Herbie to go to where these sounds had originated, and he began thinking of ways to combine his flute with the exotic rhythms of Africa.

9

THE EVOLUTION OF MANN

It took a few months before Herbie Mann began combining percussion with his flute in his performing groups. He had a lucrative career going for him as a studio musician, and initially, after the *Orgy in Rhythm* session was completed, he continued on as if nothing had happened. But further innovations in 1957 showed evidence that Herbie was already exploring new avenues for his flute playing.

Two weeks after the Blakey session, A. K. Salim, a saxophonist and arranger best known for his scoring for big bands during the forties, wrote *Flute Suite* for Herbie and Frank Wess. Born Albert Atkinson in 1922, Salim converted to Islam in the 1940s, changing his name to Ahmad Khatab Salim. A jaw injury in 1943 resulted in his retirement as a performer, and from then on, he worked strictly as an arranger. For the next five years, he wrote for a variety of big bands, including those of Lucky Millinder, Jimmie Lunceford, and Lionel Hampton. After the American Federation of Musicians' 1948 strike broke up many of the big bands, Salim returned to working with smaller groups. His arrangements, rooted in blues, also included work in Latin idioms, making his work attractive to bandleaders like Machito, Tito Puente, and Dizzy Gillespie.

Frank Wess first added the flute to his arsenal in 1954, when he was playing with Count Basie. *Flute Suite*, which was released on Savoy, featured six tightly arranged blues-influenced charts that permitted Herbie and Wess to improvise both individually and as a duo, on flute as well as tenor sax. Herbie was particularly effective on alto flute on "Miltown Blues." The two were accompanied by trumpeter Joe Wilder, trombonist Frank Rehak, pianist Hank Jones, bassist Wendell Marshall, and drummer Bobby Donaldson.

The late 1950s found Herbie altruistically working with other flute players on the jazz scene. On his next project, recorded for Prestige, he joined forces with Belgian hard-bop saxophonist Bobby Jaspar, an agile, imaginative flutist himself. The album, titled *Flute Soufflé*, featured a tune where Herbie, for the first time, looked to his own cultural background for inspiration. "Tel Aviv" featured a brooding, dirgelike melody that Herbie played on alto flute before giving way to Jaspar's Stan Getz--influenced tenor sax solo. "Purposely, I wanted to write a song that expressed my heritage," Herbie later recalled. "I really like that song. Bobby Jaspar's tenor sax and the flute sound really nice together."

Expanding his musical flexibility even further, Herbie played bass clarinet on his next album, *Sultry Serenade*, on which he began adding horns to his group, using Urbie Green on trombone and Jack Nimitz on baritone sax and bass clarinet in a Riverside session produced by Orrin Keepnews. This practice continued shortly afterward with the Epic Records release *Salute to the Flute*, which featured a big band with three trumpets, two trombones, and three saxophones.

In May, Herbie finished off Salim's *Flute Suite* with three tunes (minus Wess) backed by another group featuring saxophonist Phil Woods, who had last heard Herbie when he was still Herbie Solomon, jamming in Brooklyn bars. Woods noticed a marked improvement in Herbie's chops and heard him for the first time on flute as well as tenor sax. Two weeks later, the band returned to the Savoy studios to record the album *Yardbird Suite*. "He'd come a long way since Tony's on Flatbush Avenue, that's for sure," Woods recalled. "He was a good tenor player, but I really think he found his voice on the flute."

On May 9, Herbie recorded *Mann Alone*, an album featuring unaccompanied flute and alto flute that *DownBeat* called a "tour de force," complimenting Herbie for his stellar musicianship and the eight original tunes he composed for the record, released on Savoy. The songs, performed extemporaneously without written scores, ran the gamut of Herbie's emotions, from swinging ("Happy Happy") to moody ("Looking Thru the Window"), the latter exhibiting Herbie's impressions of a somber day looking outside of his Greenwich Village apartment.

A late-night stroll home from a nightclub engagement prompted the walking blues "From Midnight On," while "Ruth, Ruth" was written for his new wife. In the summer, Herbie spent a few months in California, still looking for new trails to blaze, but was unsure which direction he wanted to go. Characteristically, he went in all directions at once, willing to try anything so long as it was new and different.

> When I came out to the West Coast, I called up Pete Rugolo, and he got me an apartment in Westwood where he was below me and André Previn was above me. Then Pete tried to get me on as many record dates as I could. So while I was there, I did about four of his albums and three or four of my own.

Los Angeles was the center of the new "West Coast" jazz sound, typified by recordings made on the Pacific Jazz and Contemporary labels. Buddy Collette described it as a "lighter sound," which emphasized heavily arranged music—but Collette also meant something else. In a 1995 interview, Collette pointed out that the sound focused on members of Local 47, the white union in town, characterized by such musicians as Gerry Mulligan, Shorty Rogers, Chet Baker, and Shelly Manne, in an attempt by West Coast record labels to market a "clean, bright" sound to reflect the sun-swept beaches of California. Collette recalled that the first-call flute player for West Coast sessions was usually someone like Bud Shank or Harry Klee. Collette, who was black, would only get gigs when white flutists were unavailable.

One of these West Coast records, *Great Ideas of Western Mann*, was a pun on the slogan of the Container Corporation of America, which had been producing a successful series of advertisements using the phrase "great ideas of Western man." The title also reflected the album's novel approach, as Herbie played the entire date on bass clarinet, an novel idea that took advantage of West Coast arrangers like Pete Rugolo, Bill Holman, and Russ Garcia, who often used rarely used instruments like flute, oboe, bassoon, and French horn in their arrangements. (It wasn't the first time Herbie recorded on the instrument. He played it on Hoagy Carmichael's "Lazy Bones," which was included on the Riverside LP *Sultry Serenade*.) Herbie was backed by a quartet of top Los Angeles session men: Jack Sheldon on trumpet, Jimmy Rowles on piano, Buddy Clark on bass, and Mel Lewis on drums. In addition, the album marked Riverside Records' entry into recording on the West Coast, cut on July 3 at Capitol Records' gleaming new tower on Vine Street, designed to look like a stack of records. Herbie used the same rhythm section of Rowles, Clark, and Lewis on his next LP, *Flute Fraternity*, on which he was paired with Buddy Collette, who traded licks with Herbie on flute, alto flute, clarinet, and saxophone.

While in Los Angeles, Herbie signed a three-album deal to record for Norman Granz's Verve label, the first contract he had committed to since his initial one with Bethlehem. Herbie recalled, "Barney Kessel decided that Verve should try to become more commercial, but he had to convince Norman Granz, who wasn't, isn't, and never was a fan of mine. We used Howard Roberts on guitar, Jimmy Rowles, Mel Lewis, and Buddy Clark, and Frank DeVol directed the strings."

Eight songs were recorded over the first two days of the session, held sometime during August, but it was the third day that proved to be the most important one of Herbie Mann's career to that point. The group that recorded that day consisted of two guitars, bass, drums, and a *conguero* named Frank "Guico" Guerrero. Guerrero's inclusion marked the first major change in Herbie's sound. One song in particular sparked the interest of New York disc jockey "Symphony Sid" Torin. A longtime bebop fan, Torin was responsible for introducing thousands of New York radio listeners to jazz. In 1957, he was broadcasting a program on WEVD-AM/FM that focused on the new wave of Latin jazz typified by artists such as Tito Puente, Mario Bauzá, and Machito. When Torin heard Herbie's debut LP for Verve, *The Magic Flute of Herbie Mann*, he was immediately drawn to one track that he played over and over on his radio program. The track, copiously titled "Evolution of Man(n)," was another multileveled pun that Herbie explained:

There was a photo book out called *The Evolution of Man*. It was a very successful paperback, a large photo book with award-winning photos in it. So that's where I got the title from. I picked the tunes and organized the musicians. Laurindo Almeida helped me with those tunes that he played on: "Frenesi," "Baia," "Peanut Vendor," and "Evolution of Man(n)." On "Evolution of Man(n)," I played a wooden flute that an Italian shoemaker from Brooklyn made for me. I made up this little melody and it was just me and percussion. After Symphony Sid started playing it, I started getting more gigs, and then I got weeklong gigs, outside of just Monday nights. It was now becoming obvious that my future was not in Charlie Parker. It was in Tito Puente, Machito, and Antônio Carlos Jobim.

In Latin music, the flute had a major role. That was really it. Also, truthfully, I found the rhythms more exciting. Straight-ahead music is in a box. It's "one-two" or "one-two-three-four." Ethnic music is in a circle. There's a lot more anticipation and there are a lot more parts. It bubbles more for me. I never really felt comfortable just playing straight ahead. For me, it's my least favorite genre.

With Symphony Sid's help and hearing the music and hearing the audience reacting to it, it made it a lot easier to just take the jump. He was the one who recommended that I add Latin percussion to the band. My first rhythm section was, I think, Chino Pozo and Candido, and then Machito's rhythm section, which was Patato and José Mangual.

Herbie Mann's employing Latin percussionists not only instantly changed his sound but opened up his own improvising abilities to reflect the techniques he first heard on Esy Morales's "Jungle Fantasy." By 1958, he was experimenting with different and exotic percussion instruments and was thinking about writing an extended work utilizing these instruments. As with everything Herbie did, there was a business angle to accompany the creative decision. At the end of his contract with Verve, he put these ideas to work in a project that would change his life as well as the direction of jazz.

10

"PAY ME IN FRONT OF MARIO AND MACHITO"

In August 1957, Herbie Mann was still stuck in the cocoon of jazz lounges and recording studios, making records as a sideman and performing in New York nightclubs. But for the first time, he was beginning to understand that to break through to mainstream audiences, he had to relate to audiences other than hardcore jazz fans. The first thing he did was change his image. With his horn-rimmed glasses and Van Dyke beard, Herbie looked like a typical Greenwich Village bopster, so he got fitted for contact lenses. He still wore his glasses, but they made fewer and fewer appearances in his performances in the next few years.

In late 1957, Herbie wrote scores for various television programs and attended a record date backing singer Tony Bennett. Bennett was recording the last of several sessions that resulted in his Columbia album *The Beat of My Heart*, a record that would help him transcend his image and be seen as a versatile jazz singer and not just a melodramatic singer of soaring Tin Pan Alley ballads. For the last day of the session, pianist/arranger Ralph Sharon hired five flutists, including Herbie, Bobby Jasper, Spencer Sinatra, Bill Slapin, and Vincent Vittorio, to record five songs, accompanied only by Bennett, Sharon, drummer Billy Exiner, and two percussionists, Candido and Sabu. Herbie and the two percussionists also joined Bennett for a gig at New York's Copacabana nightclub the following February.

On his next record date, Herbie played on an album of straight-ahead jazz with guitarist Kenny Burrell. In addition, he played sax in a septet led by clarinetist Buddy DeFranco and cut a few tracks with Michel Legrand's orchestra on his *Legrand Jazz* album. The album featured a veritable all-star lineup, including Miles Davis, John Coltrane, Paul Chambers, and Herbie's old Brooklyn pal, Phil Woods. Woods recalled:

> I remember Bill Evans was there, too. Michel was not playing piano that day, thank God. We used to call him "Busy Fingers." A great musician, but not a great pianist. But Miles and Coltrane were there with us. Man, that was a thrill, sitting between those two cats. But I knew them pretty well. When you're in New York and you're playing Birdland all the time, you get to meet all of the giants.

At the end of the year, Herbie won his first *DownBeat* Readers Poll, finishing ahead of Bud Shank, Frank Wess, and Buddy Collette. He would win every year after that until 1970, an unbroken string of thirteen straight years. But he would never find favor with music critics, consistently finishing lower in those polls.

Late in 1958, Herbie was hired by Mario Bauzá to write songs for a new album he was readying for Roulette Records. Bauzá was the longtime musical director for the Afro-Cuban orchestra fronted by Francisco "Machito" Grillo, the Havana-born musician who was one of the chief pioneers of Afro-Cuban jazz. It was at this session that Herbie realized how to adapt his rhythm section to best complement his flute. He recalled:

> When I was with Mat and then with Pete Rugolo and Tony Bennett, with the exception of a few Latin-tinged tunes, it was all straight-ahead. When I formed my first band, that's the music we were playing. I was doing Monday nights at Birdland, and Symphony Sid told me, "Latin jazz is a very big thing in New York. Why don't you add some Latin percussionists to your band?" So I played the same music—"I Remember April," "Summertime," "Caravan," "A Night in Tunisia"—but added the Latin instruments. All of a sudden, the audience had a point of reference, especially New York audiences, because in a Latin band, the flute players were the improvisers. And they'd say, "Ohhh, the flute! That's right. It's with conga drums and bongos and timbales." That was the third

stepping-stone for me. First came Benny Goodman, then Mat Mathews, and then Symphony Sid suggesting Latin jazz.

I played Birdland a lot. I did a week with the Machito band and then did the Roulette album with them, which had Johnny Griffin on tenor and Curtis Fuller on trombone. It was originally called *Machito with Flute to Boot*. I wrote all the arrangements and all the tunes, but I was just the featured player. As my popularity grew, Machito's name got less and less prominent on the cover. Today it's on the Garland label as *On the Prowl* by Herbie Mann with no mention of Machito at all.

The Machito orchestra was the chief catalyst for the combining of jazz and Latin music in the 1940s and 1950s, one of the earliest examples of jazz "fusion." For the first time, Herbie Mann employed techniques he learned from Esy Morales's "Jungle Fantasy" on a full-length album, not just isolated tracks, as he had been doing since the beginning of his career. The Machito band provided Herbie the opportunity to hire Latin percussionists to add to his group.

Herbie's new group made its debut early in June 1959 at New York's Basin Street East, a plush nightclub off Lexington Avenue in Manhattan. The club, which had formerly been called Casa Cugat, already had a strong Afro-Cuban history, and with Herbie's existing fans coming across town from Birdland, the new group became an instant hit. Herbie's second Verve album was recorded there on June 30, which showed the radical direction his sound had taken since his debut with the label nearly two years earlier. At the end of the concert, Herbie announced that the album would be titled *Jazz Primitive*, but by the time it was issued later that year, it was being called *Flautista!* with the subtitle "Herbie Mann Plays Afro-Cuban Jazz." The album was the first of many live recordings Herbie made during his career, a format he favored because it added the element of audience enthusiasm to maximize the effect of his music.

Herbie's new sound focused on the combination of the flute and vibraphone, which replaced the flute-guitar-rhythm formula he had been using since his first Bethlehem session in 1954. On vibes was John Anthony Pompeo, aka Johnny Rae, a California-born musician of Italian ancestry who had played with the George Shearing Quintet and guitarist Johnny

Smith's quartet, both straight-ahead bebop groups. The flute-and-vibes sound would become a staple of Herbie's bands through the early 1970s, with a procession of top-flight vibraphonists succeeding Rae.

On percussion were three musicians hired from the Machito band: the diminutive (at four feet, eight inches tall) Cuban Carlos "Patato" Valdes, on conga drums, and two cousins from Puerto Rico: Jose Luis Mangual on bongos and Santos Miranda on drums and timbales. Nabil "Knobby" Totah, who was born in Palestine, rounded out the group on bass, making it one of the first American jazz bands predominantly constructed from non-U.S. natives.

On *Flautista!*'s first song, "Todos Locos," Herbie introduced a newly designed flute keyed in E-flat, a minor third higher than the conventional C flute, which had a higher-pitched sound that Herbie likened to that of the Cuban-derived *charanga* flute, a wooden instrument that is a cross between a flute, a fife, and a piccolo, and which is an octave higher than the flute. "I was thinking of Bud Powell's composition 'Un Poco Loco,' meaning a little crazy," Herbie said in the album's liner notes. "It has that sort of don't-give-a-damn attitude, designed to show off the character of this particular instrument at an up tempo."

To accentuate his new fusion of jazz and world music, Herbie made sure to encourage his musicians to use native instruments on his records and in concert whenever possible. On "Amazon River," Herbie played a homemade cane flute crafted in Argentina, one of many such instruments from his ever-expanding collection of world flutes. Valdes, Mangual, and Miranda played a set of three small, tuned Kenya drums, while Rae played marimba and Totah manipulated finger cymbals.

DownBeat was ecstatic about the new sound. The publication caught up with Herbie's group at the Village Gate in Greenwich Village. The reviewer noted that Herbie's instruments included his standard flute, various wooden flutes from other cultures, and bass clarinet, the latter played on the loping "Come On Mule." "His unusual septet got to swinging like mad," *DownBeat* raved. The acclaim for the new group was such that Herbie was immediately booked for a week at the Apollo Theater and another at the Half Note.

When *Flautista!* was finally released early in 1960, *DownBeat* reviewer Don DeMichael said, "If this LP doesn't make you shake your posterior, nothing will. Possessed of a fire and a lilting, dancing quality that can become hypnotic, this hell-for-leather group swings from the word 'go.'"

Herbie was always known for being extremely generous to his musicians, not only allowing them to play what they felt in their performances, but also paying them better than any other bandleader in town. He smiled impishly when he recalled:

The Latin bandleaders in New York *hated* me. They were paying these guys forty-five dollars a night, and I was paying them a hundred and fifty. So I was stealing their rhythm sections. I remember a funny story once. We played a gig at City Center, and on the show was the Machito band. So I get ready to pay Patato and he says, 'Pay me in front of Mario and Machito.' So I said, 'Patato, here!' And I started peeling off bills. "Twenty, forty, sixty, eighty, one hundred. Twenty, forty . . . " Mario stops me and yells, 'Oh, no! What's happening?' Patato says, 'Respect.'"

11

AFRICAN SUITE

In November 1958, Herbie began working on a project he called "African Suite." He had recently left the Machito band, where he had been a featured soloist, and had formed another group, using several of Machito's percussionists. Herbie's creation, however, had an ulterior motive: he wanted to go on a tour of Africa and had discussed the matter with noted jazz historian Dr. Marshall Stearns, who was on the advisory panel to the International Cultural Exchange program, established by President Eisenhower. According to Herbie, he told Stearns he wanted "to show the Africans how much our American jazz music owes to its African heritage."

The group he would take along "would be designed to demonstrate the roots of jazz in African tribal music and show how the evolution of jazz reflects the tempo and rhythms of American life, with its form and spirit remaining basically African."

The racial makeup of Herbie's band, however, was the cause of some concern. Herbie noted that clarinetist Tony Scott had complained that the ICE program committee had told him not to include blacks in his band when making a similar trip to the Middle East. As a result, an all-white band led by Jack Teagarden was substituted for Scott's mixed-race group. New Orleans jazz trombonist Wilbur De Paris was the most recent musician to tour Africa, taking another all-white group of New Orleans musicians on a State Department--sponsored tour that lasted from March to May 1957.

When it was Herbie's turn, he was vehement about using a racially mixed group. "It's time that we show the European and the African visually, as well as musically, the evolutionary process where men with different backgrounds live together and produce something artistically worthwhile."

Stearns presented Herbie's plan to the panel and an audition was set up at the Village Gate. As part of his proposal, Herbie presented his completed "African Suite," which demonstrated the musical fusion of jazz with African rhythms. Consisting of four movements—"Bedouin," "Sudan," "Ekunda," and "Guinean"—the suite sought to combine his flute with the propulsive percussion heard in native African cultures. As he explained:

> Every culture, except ours, has some kind of flute and percussion in its history, even Native American cultures. The first instrument was a percussion instrument and the second instrument was a flutelike kind of instrument, because it didn't take any great mental process to just put a bunch of holes in a piece of wood, a piece of cane, or a bone. I was not attempting to put down exactly what I heard in African music, but to interpret the sounds of what I heard through my jazz background. Before I left for Africa, I listened to field recordings. I wanted to show them how their music came here, what I did with it, and then bring it back. But first I needed to hear and see the music for myself.

The album featuring "African Suite" was recorded during the summer of 1959 and released on the United Artists label. Because Herbie was currently contracted to Verve, the album was credited to "Johnny Rae's Afro-Jazz Septet." The four-movement suite took up one side of the LP. On the other side, Herbie included an Afro-Cuban version of Sonny Rollins's calypso-flavored "St. Thomas" and "Sorimaó," which Herbie played on bass clarinet. (*DownBeat*'s curmudgeonly John S. Wilson likened the sound to "a drain pipe in heat.") Rounding out the album was what Wilson described as a "gut-ripping" version of Esy Morales's "Jungle Fantasy," Herbie's first recording of the fiery rumba that had inspired him to take up the flute in the first place. Wilson liked the fact that Herbie used drummer Philly Joe Jones, bassist Jack Six, and drummer

Bob Corwin in the ensemble, which gave Herbie's flute "the lift it needs to strip it of the insipid, plodding qualities the instrument has in the usual jazz surroundings." The album notes were written by Symphony Sid, who described the enthusiastic response of listeners during Herbie's appearances with the Machito band.

When it was completed, the album was submitted by the American National Theater and Academy to the seventeen American consuls in Africa. Eleven consular posts accepted Herbie's proposal immediately, but the remaining six doubted that Africans would appreciate such "sophisticated" music. In response, ANTA also sent copies of Herbie's previous Verve effort, *Flautista!* but the consuls still did not budge. In a position contrary to that of the consuls, ANTA thought the music Herbie was proposing was too primitive for Africans and advised him to add more traditional jazz instruments to the group. Herbie later said:

> The State Department decided, in their infinite wisdom, that African-based music would not go across with Africans, so I had to add two instruments, trumpet and trombone. The State Department had lots of people from the South, and they thought that Dixieland was jazz. So I added Doc Cheatham on trumpet and Jimmy Knepper on trombone. [Note: Knepper never made the tour; he was replaced by Willie Dennis.]

ANTA's reasoning for adding the horns was because they wanted Herbie's band to be versatile enough to play a variety of American jazz styles, including Dixieland, swing, and bebop, as well as Afro-Cuban. Herbie felt that the six dissenting consuls merely wanted him to put on shows for their private parties, rather than display any kind of public relations statement about "sharing cultural ideas." His fears proved to be accurate in some instances.

Herbie played selections from "African Suite" during his initial nightclub appearances with his new group during the summer of 1959. One song, "Bedouin," which featured Herbie playing a Japanese flute against an insistent 12/8 groove, was played during his first appearance at the Newport Folk Festival on the afternoon of July 4, four days after the live recording at Basin Street East. Herbie's sextet played four songs that day, with the percolating percussion section highlighting the set. After the last song, "Brazilian Soft Shoe" from the Machito album, the Newport crowd gave the group a rousing ovation, shouting, "More! More!" Rae was about to roll his vibes off the stage, but someone can be heard saying, "Not yet, Johnny!" Herbie then introduced Duke Ellington's "Caravan," a vibrant ten-minute-long world-music jam. By the time of Herbie's next appearance on the Newport stage four years later, he would be a worldwide sensation.

In late 1959, the State Department finally approved the tour of Africa, and Herbie and his band departed on the last day of the year. Two weeks before they left, the consul post in Senegal, the group's first stop, changed its mind and pulled out. Herbie and the band thus spent the first four days of their tour lolling on a beach at Dakar.

The tour lasted fourteen weeks, running from December 31, 1959, to April 5, 1960, with visits to Sierra Leone, Liberia, Nigeria, Angola, Mozambique, the Rhodesia/Nyasaland Federation, Tanganyika, Kenya, Uganda, Ethiopia, Sudan, Morocco, and Tunisia. Herbie later said wryly, "We would have played the Congo, but Lumumba and his guys were sharpening their knives."

They traveled through the jungles by bus and into the copper belt by railway. Concerts were played everywhere, from remote villages to swanky private clubs. Of the $4,600 weekly budget, two-thirds of the money went to pay the musicians. Herbie earned $1,200 per week. The other musicians earned the following: Johnny Rae (vibes), $350; Patato Valdes (*conguero*) and Jose Mangual (bongos), $325 each; Doc Cheatham (trumpet) and Willie Dennis (trombone), $300 each, and Don Payne (bass), $275. (Drummer Rudy Collins rounded out the octet, but was not listed on the payroll manifest.)

Time magazine did a story on Herbie's tour, titled "Jazz in the Jungle," and reported that Herbie's band played to a steady succession of sold-out houses, "jammed with both European jazz enthusiasts and native tribesmen who recognize in Mann's percussive style the distant echoes of their own primitive jungle beat." Herbie acquired twenty different native flutes and a variety of percussion instruments during his travels. He delighted in playing as many different kinds of instruments as possible, including his assortment of flutes, the tenor sax, clarinet, and bass clarinet.

In addition to performing, the musicians listened to as much native music as they could, learning melodic and rhythmic ideas that Herbie used to craft additional compositions after returning to the U.S.

In Nairobi, Kenya, British journalists became suspicious of the Americans because of the U.S. government's opposition to England's efforts to thwart the so-called Mau Mau rebellion against British colonialism. More than one Englishman heckled Herbie with statements like "We were here before the Africans." In one interview, a British journalist asked Herbie, "Is your tour a musical one?" When Herbie responded that he was only trying to show the Africans and Europeans they could live with one another, the reporter responded, "That's what I mean. You people are always interfering in the internal problems of other countries."

In a jam session with the royal flutist in Buganda, a subnational kingdom within Uganda, Herbie was ceremoniously presented with a handmade flute, a scene repeated in many African nations. Many Africans wondered how Herbie had learned their rhythms so well. Herbie recalled how he opened each concert: "We'd start the gigs by playing 'Caravan.' I'd play it in three different styles, then check out the audience to see which one they liked. And then the rest of the program was based on which style they liked."

Selections from all of America's jazz eras were played. New Orleans jazz was represented by "When the Saints Go Marching In" and "Struttin' with Some Barbecue." Swing-era songs included Bunny Berigan's "I Can't Get Started," Benny Goodman's "A Smooth One," and Lionel Hampton's "Flying Home." Count Basie numbers like "Lester Leaps In" and "Tickle Toe" were also audience favorites. The shows often closed with Dizzy Gillespie's "A Night in Tunisia," highlighted by a five-minute drum solo by Rudy Collins.

In Addis Ababa, the capital of Ethiopia, the group jammed with the Imperial Guard band of Emperor Haile Selassie. In Salisbury, Northern Rhodesia, students from classical music schools came to hear Herbie's group play at the Rhodes National Art Gallery, the first time a musical performance had ever been held there. At the gallery, Herbie's band played directly under a famous Gobelin tapestry, one of many priceless artifacts that lined the walls of the main hall.

In Mozambique, Herbie was particularly fascinated but mystified by a primitive flute that had been crafted in Mombasa, Kenya, from bamboo, bound with copper wire with the tone holes burned into its side. No matter how hard he tried, Herbie could not get a sound out of the instrument. He bought the flute from its owner on the spot, determined to master it.

During the tour, bassist Don Payne became engaged to an English autograph seeker five days after they had met. They were married after the conclusion of the tour.

After it was all over, an exultant Herbie said, "The tour proved to me that the idea about presenting African rhythms was right. I felt that if you give people something that they can identify with, then you can progress from there and carry them some of the way with you."

For Herbie, the inclusion of the African percussion instruments convinced him that the key to expanding his audience beyond the small New York jazz nightclubs was to use African-derived percussion. The response of the African audiences to hearing American jazz accented by native instruments made him realize how to do this. He had found a purpose for his flute: "riding on top of the waves" of indigenous rhythm sections like a surfer on a surf board, attracting listeners from one culture to another. It was the key inspirational moment of his career.

12

THE COMMON GROUND

One month to the day after he returned to the U.S., Herbie was back in the studio recording his third and final album for Verve. Herbie already knew he wanted to sign with Atlantic Records, where he would have a sympathetic ear in Atlantic's head of jazz, Nesuhi Ertegun, so he used his final Verve album as an "audition" record to pitch to Ertegun.

Born in 1917, Nesuhi Ertegun became a student of American jazz after arriving in 1939 from his native Turkey with his family, led by his father, the Turkish ambassador to the United States. Both Nesuhi and his younger brother Ahmet were enamored with American jazz, and religiously attended jazz concerts in Washington, D.C., where they lived with their parents. By the age of twenty-three, Nesuhi was already a respected and knowledgeable authority on early New Orleans jazz.

In 1946, Nesuhi married Marili Morden, proprietor of the Jazz Man Record Shop, a collector's store in Hollywood that specialized in selling traditional jazz 78s. The couple ran the store together as well as its eponymous record label, which pioneered the New Orleans jazz revival of the 1940s, led by releases by trumpeter Lu Watters and New Orleans jazz pioneer Bunk Johnson. In 1952, Ertegun and Morden divorced. Three years later, Ertegun joined his brother as a partner in Atlantic Records, which Ahmet had founded in 1947. Nesuhi was put in charge of establishing the label's jazz division, and in a matter of only a few years, signed a stellar roster of stars that would eventually include Shorty Rogers, Lennie Tristano, Lee Konitz, John Coltrane,

Charles Mingus, Ray Charles, Ornette Coleman, and the Modern Jazz Quartet.

Herbie knew that Nesuhi Ertegun would be receptive to his ideas of fusing world music with jazz and was glad to be getting a chance to leave Norman Granz, who was mainly a traditionalist and didn't care for Herbie's new experiments. Herbie recalled:

> Monte Kay, my manager, also managed Chris Connor, who recorded for Atlantic, and he negotiated the deal for me. I didn't produce my own records until the second or third contract. The first ones were done by Nesuhi Ertegun. But there was incredible freedom and input. I picked all the tunes and he was my first sergeant in the booth. Actually, I signed with Atlantic before going to Africa. We didn't record until I got back.

Four musicians who accompanied Herbie to Africa—Knobby Totah, Rudy Collins, Johnny Rae, and Doc Cheatham—were used on the final Verve album, which was unimaginatively titled *Flute, Brass, Vibes & Percussion*. To this, he added three more trumpets—Siggy Schatz, Jerome Kail, and Leo Ball—forming a powerful choir of the horns that *conguero* Ray Mantilla called "the screaming trumpets." Along with Mantilla, the percussion section was further strengthened by the addition of the jazz-minded Ray Barretto on bongos. Mantilla recalled:

> I had played the Latin/salsa scene for twenty years. I had played with José Curbelo, Pupi Campo, and others, but then I met Ray Barretto. Ray was into the jazz scene, playing bebop conga drums. I met him one day in the Bronx and we liked each other, so we started to jam. So I got him involved in the Latin scene and he got me involved with the jazz scene. One of the first things he got me on was with Arnett Cobb on "Flying Home Mambo." Then he ended up going with Tito Puente. One day he calls me up and says, "Look, I'm with Tito now, but you've got to take this gig with Herbie Mann until I'm ready to leave." He wanted me to hold the gig for him. So I went with Herbie and started to do well with him. Patato and Mangual had just come back from Africa with him, and we did the

Herbie Mann's grandfather, Rabbi Samuel Brecher. Courtesy of Judi Solomon Kennedy.

Herbie's parents: Harry Solomon and Ruth Brecher Solomon. Courtesy of Judi Solomon Kennedy.

Herbie Solomon, age nine, with his cousin, Renee Klein Gottlieb, Brooklyn, 1939. Courtesy of Judi Solomon Kennedy.

Herbie, ten, and his sister Judi, three, at Brighton Beach, Brooklyn, 1940. Courtesy of Judi Solomon Kennedy.

Ruth and Harry Solomon (*left*) celebrate their fiftieth wedding anniversary with their children, Herbie and Judi, September 1976. Courtesy of Judi Solomon Kennedy.

A confident and now worldly Herbie in Italy, c. 1950. Courtesy of MCG Jazz.

Army recruit Herbie Solomon, age nineteen, in 1949. Courtesy of MCG Jazz.

Playing tenor with a jazz combo in Trieste. Courtesy of Janeal Arison.

On a rare detail. Courtesy of Janeal Arison.

Playing clarinet with the Army band, February 1951. Courtesy of Janeal Arison.

"Bop Solomon" (*top row, far right*), in the Army basketball team photo, February 1951. Herbie's own caption in his scrapbook identified himself as "George Mikan," in honor of the Minneapolis Lakers' bespectacled center. Courtesy of Janeal Arison.

Hanging out with some buddies on the base in Trieste. Herbie is at the right. Courtesy of Janeal Arison.

Having fun with a pal while on furlough in Paris, May 1951. Courtesy of Janeal Arison.

Esy Morales (1916–1950), composer of "Jungle Fantasy." From the author's collection.

1953 Brunswick 45 EP from the first session by the Mat Mathews Quintet. From the author's collection.

Morales's 1947 recording of "Jungle Fantasy," which inspired Herbie to take up the flute. From the author's collection.

Herbie Mann's first album, *East Coast Jazz/4* (1954), autographed to the author on November 30, 1999. Herbie's inscription reads: "Best Wishes. Thanks for the interest. I'll see you at 75"—he never made it. From the author's collection.

From Herbie Mann's first recording session, a January 1953 session with the Mat Mathews Quintet, backing Carmen McRae. From the author's collection.

Recording *Mann in the Morning* in Stockholm, Sweden, October 12, 1956. *L–R* are the front line of the Arne Domnérus Septet: Lennart Jansson, baritone sax; Arne Domnérus, alto sax; Herbie on tenor, Rolf Blomqvist, tenor sax; and Bengt-Arne Walling, trumpet. Photo by Bengt Malmqvist. Courtesy of Janeal Arison.

The Mat Mathews Quartet recording for Elektra, 1957. *L–R*: Joe Puma, Whitey Mitchell, Mat Mathews, Herbie Mann. From the author's collection.

Mann Alone, Herbie Mann's unaccompanied flute album, recorded for Savoy on May 9, 1957. From the author's collection.

Working out arrangements in his home studio, c. 1959. Courtesy of Janeal Arison.

Herbie, at the time he was adding exotic percussion instruments to his band at Basin Street East, c. June 1959. Courtesy of Janeal Arison.

Jazz Flutist Really Gets Off The Brooklyn Launching Pad

By WILLIAM PEPER,
World-Telegram Staff Writer.

When it's far out you want to go, Brooklyn seems to be a good place for the launching pad.

In 1918 Herbie Mann was a member of the school band at Abraham Lincoln High School. Next month he'll be playing a jazz flute accompanied by a couple of Afro-Cuban drummers at a state ball in Nigeria. How far out can you go?

Mr. Mann is the first flutist to make a career as a jazz musician and on Dec. 28 he and his band will go off on a three-and-a-half-month tour of Africa under the auspices of the American National Theater and Academy and the United States Department's Cultural Exchange Program.

Started at 6.

Mr. Mann, 29, started playing the piano when he was 6 and took up the clarinet and sax when he was nine. He was 15 when he began studying the flute.

He didn't start playing jazz until he was well out of Brooklyn. That began when he was

HERBIE MANN.

a member of the 98th Army Band in Trieste, Italy.

Today he says he wants to be to the flute what Benny Goodman is to the clarinet.

He formed his own band in 1955 after several years with the bands of Mat Mathews and Pete Rugolo. His specialty is setting the delicate sound of the flute against vibrant Afro-Cuban rhythms.

The result has fascinated the more advanced jazz addicts in albums like "African Suite" and "Evolution of Mann."

Now in Philadelphia.

This week he is playing in a Philadelphia club but next Tuesday he returns to Manhattan to play at the Village Vanguard.

Mr. Mann left Brooklyn in 1956 when he and his wife, Ruth, took up residence in a one-room apartment in Greenwich Village. Things h a v e picked up since then and the Manns now have five rooms uptown near Central Park.

His parents, Mr. and Mrs. Harry Solomon, still live in Brooklyn on Homecrest Ave.

16 Countries.

The first stop on the African tour, which will take in 16 countries, will be Liberia, where the Herbie Mann African Jazz Sextet will play for the inaugural ball of President William Tubman.

The tour also will include Rhodesia, Kenya, Morocco and Ethiopia, where the group will play for Emperor Haile Selassie.

Article in the *New York World-Telegram* announcing Herbie's trip to Africa, late 1959. Courtesy of Janeal Arison.

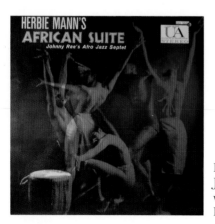

The lean and handsome Herbie, now wearing contact lenses, exuded confidence and professionalism in this 1957 photo. From the author's collection.

Herbie Mann's *African Suite* had to be credited to vibist Johnny Rae because Herbie was still signed to Verve when he made the record in the summer of 1959. From the author's collection.

Herbie Mann's Afro-Jazz Septet, 1959. Herbie, in front (with flute and pith helmet). The percussionists are Carlos "Patato" Valdes (*below*), and Rudy Collins (*middle*). Standing, *left to right*: Willie Dennis, trombone; Jose Mangual, drums; Don Payne, bass; Booker Little, trumpet; Johnny Rae, vibraphone. Courtesy of Janeal Arison.

Herbie and his first wife, Ruth, greet dignitaries at an unspecified location during his African tour, 1960. Courtesy of Janeal Arison.

Herbie in Uganda, 1960, with musicians of the *kabaka* (king) of Buganda, a kingdom within Uganda. Courtesy of Janeal Arison.

Marquee in Lourenço Marques, capital city of Mozambique, 1960. Courtesy of Janeal Arison.

Herbie Mann's Afro-Jazz Group, performing at the home of Mr. and Mrs. Pat Belcher in the exclusive Ikoyi neighborhood in Lagos, Nigeria, the first leg of their African tour, January 1960. L–R: Jose Mangual, bongos; Rudy Collins, drums (*in rear*); Jimmy Knepper, trombone, Doc Cheatham, trumpet; Don Payne, bass (*in rear*); Johnny Rae, vibraphone; and Herbie on flute. Photo by Anthony A. Udochi. Courtesy of Janeal Arison.

Taking a break for a photo op at an airport, possibly in Bulawayo, Zimbabwe, 1960. L–R: Doc Cheatham, trumpet; Don Payne, bass; Carlos "Patato" Valdes, conga drums; Jimmy Knepper, trombone; Johnny Rae, vibraphone; Jose Mangual, bongos; Herbie; and Rudy Collins, drums. Courtesy of Janeal Arison.

Théatre Municipal de Tunis

Pour la première fois à Tunis
L'une des meilleures formations de Jazz Américain

HERBIE MANN

et son Orchestre

avec

CARLOS VALDEZ - JOSE LUIS MANGUAL
JOHN RAE - DON PAYNE - RUDDIE COLLINS
WILLIE DENNIS - DOC CHEATHAN

Dimanche 3 Avril : Soirée à 21 h.
PRIX DES PLACES : 850 - 650 - 450 et 250 millimes

Lundi 4 Avril : Matinée à 18 h. 15
PRIX DES PLACES : 850 - 650 - 450 et 250 Millimes

Prix spéciaux pour Etudiants et Membres des Associations de Jeunesses

IMP. LA FLECHE - TUNIS

Rare poster of Herbie Mann's last performance during his African tour, at the Théâtre Municipal de Tunis in Tunisia, North Africa, April 3–4, 1960. Courtesy of Janeal Arison.

album for Verve as the Herbie Mann Nonet, with "the screaming trumpets." So I stopped doing salsa and was playing Afro-Cuban with Herbie. I was really playing the same kind of thing as I did with the Latin bands, except the music had changed. There was plenty of work all over the place. We worked fifty weeks a year. Johnny Rae was the first white guy I ever saw who could play timbales. Barretto was still with Tito, but he came to do the session with us. After that, it was like "Can you top this?" with the percussionists.

On July 2, 1960, Herbie played the Newport Jazz Festival for the second consecutive year, bringing with him a sextet, but without the trumpet choir he had used on the Verve album. By this time, he had added the colorful Nigerian drummer Babatunde Olatunji, known to his friends as Michael, to his percussion section. Olatunji had just released his album *Drums of Passion* on the Columbia label, which became a major hit, introducing many jazz fans to world-music rhythms. Herbie had a keen eye for musicians with entertainment value and was delighted to have Olatunji join his group. Ray Mantilla recalled:

> Everybody wore these thin suits back then; we all looked beautiful, but Olatunji would come out wearing these African robes and his pillbox hat, playing his three African drums. Whatever I did with Ray Barretto, we could have stood on our heads, but Olatunji was the whole show. When we played the Apollo, he tore the house down. He brought the African influence of drumming to jazz, which is actually present in all kinds of drumming. He had these huge floor-standing, shoulder-high African drums with him and he'd beat them with a huge stick. He was a colorful guy and was exploiting the interest in things African that was going on then. Michael was also an imposing figure with his traditional African robes and his big drums, and he always made a big impression. And Herbie knew it. That was part of the show business thing. Even today, it's evident in the way a lot of groups dress. But Herbie knew how to make a visual impression. Big time.

As he did at Newport in 1959, Herbie started his forty-minute set with Sonny Rollins's "St. Thomas" and then introduced Olatunji. They played "Bedouin" from "African Suite," with Johnny Rae playing a marimba from Mozambique, Olatunji's Nigerian drums, and Herbie on a Japanese flute and finger cymbals acquired from Henry Adler's drum shop in New York City. Then Herbie introduced a new song he had written with Olatunji called "Uhuru," the Swahili word for *freedom*. Herbie had written the song for his "Evolution of Jazz Suite," which he'd played on the African tour. While Olatunji sang the lyrics in Swahili, Herbie played the loping three-quarter-time melody on tenor sax. By this time, Herbie had all but abandoned the tenor sax in his act. He would only make one more record on the instrument, in 1966, but occasionally pulled it out for live performances.

Announcing his last number, Herbie ignored a cry from the audience for "Caravan" and instead played the percussion-rich "Todos Locos" from *Flautista!* Brought back for an encore, he returned to his Japanese flute for "Brazilian Soft Shoe" ("It's neither Brazilian or soft," Herbie joked to the audience), which he had also played at the 1959 festival. *The New York Times'* John S. Wilson said Herbie's Afro-jazz group "was stirred to a tremendous head of steam" by Olatunji, "whose flowing robes and decorated cap lent the group an air of authenticity."

The group continued its experiments with African rhythms at the Village Gate, a large nightclub in the basement of the old Mills Hotel in Greenwich Village. The club, owned by Art D'Lugoff, was surrounded by coffeehouses that featured mostly folk music acts at the time, so D'Lugoff tried switching to jazz for the summer months. One of the first acts he booked was Herbie Mann's Afro-Jazz Septet, featuring Olatunji and a young poet/singer named Maya Angelou. The Village Gate would become the location for Herbie's breakthrough success the following year. He began playing Monday nights shortly after D'Lugoff changed formats, and on Thanksgiving 1960, D'Lugoff booked Herbie's group for an entire week.

The final Verve album was completed in late July, and only a week later, Herbie began his twenty-year association with Atlantic Records. The label would bring him fame and fortune, but also alienate him from the jazz world, as he got more and more popular with mainstream audiences.

For his first Atlantic album, Herbie used the Verve musicians, including the "screaming trumpets" of Cheatham, Ball, Schatz, and Kail. The album emphasized music from the African tour and featured on its cover a photograph (shot by Ruth Mann) of Herbie playing flute in the doorway of a home where Kabakan flutists lived, in the Ugandan province of Buganda. Maya Angelou joined Herbie's group, singing in the background chorus.

A highlight of the album was "Sawa Sawa De," a folk song Herbie had heard sung in Sierra Leone by a group of children. He also included an Armenian melody, "Asia Minor" (a favorite of Charlie Parker), Dizzy Gillespie's "A Night in Tunisia," and two examples of Herbie's fusion of African, Afro-Cuban, and American jazz: "High Life" and a song that also became the album's title, "The Common Ground." Herbie talked about the meaning of the album's title:

> I was looking for that "common ground" to show that there was a connection with all music. So where do you go for that? You go to Africa. In all of our music, the rhythmic part comes from Africa. The harmonic part probably came from Europe. I really think that jazz as an American thing was just a fluke. What if Norway and Denmark and Sweden had the kind of agriculture where they needed slaves? Then the slaves would have gone up the fjords and jazz would have come down the fjords instead of going up the Mississippi. Not many people know this, but the first slaves that came to New Orleans were from Baia, which is in northern Brazil.

DownBeat's Barbara Gardner, however, didn't quite grasp the "common ground" connotation. Although she stated hopefully that "somewhere there is a place for an album like this," her reaction to *The Common Ground* was that it was basically an exercise in rhythms and flutes, and although she commended Herbie for presenting his collection of "imported goodies," she said there was little definable jazz in the album. She was impressed by the "stately, majestic, and happy" sound of "High Life" and the authentic sounds of "Uhuru" and "Sawa Sawa De."

DownBeat's 1960 Readers Poll once again placed Herbie at the top of the heap of jazz flutists—he almost doubled the votes of the second-place finisher, Frank Wess. The International Critics Poll, which never reflected what the readers voted on, put him in second place, far behind Wess.

Johnny Rae wanted to leave the band shortly after the first Atlantic album was completed, so Herbie hired a Canadian, Hagood Hardy, to replace him. Before leaving, Rae participated in one last session, a musical setting accompanying narrated excerpts from Walter Benton's 1943 book of poems *This Is My Beloved*, read by actor Laurence Harvey. "He wasn't even there," Mantilla recalled. "We just did the tracks and Harvey read the poems on top of our tracks." Although Hardy played vibes on the session, Rae joined Mantilla in the percussion section, playing drums to Mantilla's congas. Herbie said:

> I tried to treat the work as if I were scoring a film or a television drama. Therefore, I approached the subject as an entity, not a series of disconnected themes. I wanted to match it with an equally sensitive score. I conceived the work as if Harvey were a vocalist. My music was intended to serve as background, with simplicity the keynote.

On November 12, 1960, Herbie Mann's Afro-Jazziacs, as the band was now being called, were captured in a performance at Birdland. The concert was one of many surreptitiously recorded by Boris Rose, a familiar presence on the New York jazz scene who had been recording radio broadcasts to a home disc-cutting machine since 1940, mostly from Birdland concerts. For years, he recorded broadcasts from the famed nightclub on radio or by smuggling a concealed tape recorder into the club. Rose issued the Herbie Mann Birdland concert on an album called *Wailin' Modernist*, issued on the Alto label, which also featured other bootlegs from Rose's collection of live concerts. (The Mann release incongruously displayed a silhouette of Sonny Rollins on the album cover.) The concert featured five songs: "Walkin'," "Hoo Doo" (a corruption of Herbie's "Uhuru"), "Baghdad/Asia Minor" (featuring "the screaming trumpets,") "Evolution of Mann," and "St. Thomas." Ray Mantilla, who played conga drums that night, remembered that the brief time he spent in Herbie's band changed his career:

> Coming from a straight-ahead salsa background and then going with Herbie, all of a sudden I got more recognition, more respect, I made more money, made more records, traveled better, was treated

better . . . everything got better with him. With the Latin bands, I was just a slave. But with Herbie, me and Barretto were the top of the game. We were the best of the best. And Herbie always paid us well.

On his second Atlantic album, recorded in April 1961, Herbie introduced new variations on his Afro-Cuban sound. The album's title, *The Family of Mann*, referred to Herbie's quickly growing collection of native flutes, seventeen of which were displayed on the album cover, standing at attention, with Herbie proudly posed behind them.

Although much of the album returned to the bop he had been playing before he went to Africa, there were some new variations. On two numbers, the old Peggy Lee swing standard "Why Don't You Do Right?" and Ray Charles's "This Little Girl of Mine," he combined his flute with three violins, turning the songs into lively *charangas*. The two *charanga* sides were issued back-to-back on a 45 rpm single. *DownBeat* critic Pete Welding, however, didn't recognize the use of violins in *charanga* music, calling them "sugary decoctions" and "heavy-handed glucosity," summarizing his comments by declaring that the album's jazz content was "remarkably low." Percussionist Ray Barretto recalled:

Herbie listened to Jose Fajardo, he listened to Orquesta Aragón, he listened to all the great Cuban *charanga* flute players. Fajardo was great playing in that style. Herbie listened to everybody. Whoever played that instrument on whatever style he played it on, Herbie was a student of it.

Carryovers from the Afro-Cuban sound were still evident, including a treatment of Bobby Timmons's "Moanin'" and a hard-bop version of a traditional Yiddish tune, "Shein Vi Di Levone." "Guinean," a movement from the "African Suite," now sounded more R&B than African, despite appearances by Herbie's cane flute and newcomer Dave Pike on marimba. Pike recalled joining the group:

He heard about me when I started playing in the Village, and he sent a messenger to come to Birdland for me to try out. So I went and tried out and he said, "If you can learn how to play timbales, you've got the job." He had Willie Bobo in the band, so I learned how to play timbales from him. I played with Herbie from 1961 until the end of '64. He kept changing all the personnel except me.

It was becoming clear that Herbie was slowly evolving away from the drum-heavy sound that typified the group that went to Africa and returning to more straight-ahead jazz sounds. But there was more going on. Herbie was searching for something else. He had been playing and recording Afro-Cuban jazz for nearly two years, but the novelty was already wearing thin. In the spring of 1961, Herbie took a night off and went to the movies, where he saw a film that changed his life.

13

"I HAVE TO GO TO BRAZIL"

The movie was called *Black Orpheus*. Made in 1959 by French director Marcel Camus, the film retells the Greek legend of Orpheus, bringing it up to date by placing it in the setting of a riotous carnival celebration in Rio de Janeiro. The movie won the Grand Prize at the 1959 Cannes Film Festival and was released in the United States the following year, where it won an Oscar for Best Foreign Film. Aside from the stunning and colorful photography of Rio during its annual Carnival festival, the film was noted for its musical score, composed by Luis Bonfá and Antônio Carlos Jobim.

The most pervasive musical style in the film was the *batucada*, a percussive Brazilian mode featuring native string instruments and massive percussion sections. Five songs were in the film, the best known being Bonfá's haunting bolero "Manhã de Carnaval" and Jobim's samba "O Nossa Amor" and "Felicidade," the last an example of the new form of Brazilian popular music known as "bossa nova." Like many other Americans who saw the film, Herbie Mann was entranced.

After seeing *Black Orpheus*, I said to Monte Kay, "I really am getting very bored. The drummers are the leaders of my band and I'm a sideman. I need something more." He was forming a tour to go down to Brazil: Coleman Hawkins, Roy Eldridge, Old Man Jo Jones, Zoot Sims, Al Cohn, and Chris Connor. I told him, "I have to go." He said, "Nobody knows you." I said, "I'll go for nothing . . . I have

to go to Brazil . . . I'm going to commit musical suicide if I don't go
. . . I will go insane." And he said, "OK, you can go."

So we went down there. Seventeen-hour flight. When we got
there, everybody went to the hotel and went directly to sleep. I put
my bags upstairs and I'm down. The Brazilian reporters waiting in
the lobby asked me, "Are you with the tour?" I said, "Yes." "What do
you play?" "Flute." "What's your name?" Told them. Nobody knew
who I was. They didn't understand English and I didn't understand
Portuguese. But at least we're communicating.

The band Herbie took with him to Brazil included Ahmed Abdul-Malik
and Ben Tucker on bass, Ray Mantilla on percussion, and Dave Bailey on
drums. Abdul-Malik, who was from Sudan, brought along a short-necked
Arabic lute called an oud that he played on a Middle Eastern--flavored
song he'd written called "Ismaa." Herbie also used other members of
the tour during his sets, including Ronnie Ball on piano, Curtis Fuller
on trombone, and Zoot Sims and Al Cohn on tenor saxophones. (Fuller
didn't know what to play when his solo came around on "Ismaa," so he
incorporated a portion of Nat Adderley's "Work Song" into it.) One
concert was recorded at the Teatro Municipal in Rio de Janeiro on July
16, 1961. The record was issued in the U.S. on the FM label.

Although Herbie was the least known of the headliners at the concert,
he soon thought of a way to stand out.

I came up with this idea. Nobody knows who I am here. I
needed a song. The minute I play this song, everybody is going to
say, "Wow. He's giving us this." So we started drinking *cachaça* and
started walking around, looking for a song. We were talking among
ourselves when we found this song called "Asa Branca." We got
the sheet music. I took it back to my room and practiced it. That
night at the concert, in the middle of playing a blues solo with my
band, I stopped, put down my flute, picked up the cane flute from
"The Evolution of Mann," and started playing this song. The whole
audience stood up and started applauding. I could have been elected
president of Brazil that night.

After the concerts, I went to the Bottles Bar, heard Sérgio Mendes play, stayed up all night listening to the music, and I said to myself, "My God. This is it."

Producer/broadcaster Willis Conover accompanied the American musicians on the tour and described how a private bus took the musicians to the promoter's resort. Among the bus passengers was a teacher at one of Rio's local samba schools, who demonstrated the local rhythms, dances, and songs, assisted by fifteen native cariocas, while the bus drove past the picturesque Sugarloaf Mountain, along the Rio beaches, and into the countryside where *Black Orpheus* was filmed. With food and drink heightening the experience, the passengers were treated to a musical orgy, with Herbie and the rest of the entourage keeping rhythm by banging on glasses, ashtrays, and whatever other hard surfaces were available.

That night, Monte Kay polled the musicians and all agreed to have the Brazilian cariocas join the band onstage at the concert. Herbie's Afro-Cuban numbers were the most affected, accented by the driving rhythms of the local musicians. Conover recalled hearing Herbie mutter over and over, "I want to record with them. I'm going to fly back down here and record with them."

The experience in Brazil had a pronounced effect on Herbie's career, but in turn, Herbie became just as big a force in the development of Brazilian jazz in the 1960s. Dr. Gerard Béhague, a prolific scholar of Latin American ethnomusicology, said:

> Herbie had a positive effect, particularly with the samba jazz tradition. Herbie appeared at Catholic University in Rio in 1961 with the Tamba Trio. The Tamba Trio was one of the very first— and very popular at the time, in the early sixties—groups playing what later came to be called Brazilian jazz. So Herbie had a direct influence on those types of Brazilian musicians who were interested in developing Brazilian jazz.

It was a mutually beneficial musical love affair. Herbie soon realized that although Afro-Cuban music was exciting and had made him a popular New York attraction, the music was melodically simplistic. After visiting Brazil, Herbie realized that Brazilian music could be just as rhythmically involved as Afro-Cuban music, but it had the added advantage of producing masterpieces of melodic beauty. For him, Brazil offered the best of both worlds: intoxicating rhythms and great melodies to improvise on. Along with Stan Getz, Charlie Byrd, and Dizzy Gillespie, Herbie Mann introduced aspects of Brazilian jazz to American audiences. But he did more than that. According to Béhague, "Herbie Mann realized the importance of the flute in Brazilian music since the early twentieth century, especially in the music of Joaquim Antonio Collado da Silva, who transformed the European polka into one of the first typical kinds of popular dance music in Brazil, which was known as the maxixe."

More than any other musician who went on the 1961 tour, Herbie Mann understood the significance of what he was hearing. And he also realized that experiencing the music of Brazil firsthand was the transformative musical moment of his life.

14

AT THE VILLAGE GATE

Sometime after their trip to Africa, Herbie and Ruth Mann decided to adopt a child. Although both were physically able to become parents, for some reason they were not able to have children together, so they adopted a boy who had been born on January 12, 1961, naming him Paul Jay Mann. Herbie's sister Judi remembered, "I know they had to wait nine months to get the adoption finalized. According to New York law, the birth mother had that long to change her mind. The adoption was finalized in September 1961, and they were ecstatic." Claudia Mann, Herbie's second child, who was also adopted, recalled, "My parents went through a very hard time because they were living in constant fear that the natural mother was going to come and take him away."

When Herbie returned to the U.S. from Brazil that summer, all he could think about was the music he had heard. In the meanwhile, his Afro-Cuban sextet was still hugely popular, especially at the now jazz-oriented Village Gate nightclub in Greenwich Village. On November 17, 1961, a concert was recorded at the club that Atlantic released early in 1962. It was his second live album. By now, Herbie realized his kind of jazz was more exciting performed live than in a studio.

> It's because you're playing off an audience instead of off the musicians. Excitement to me is the criteria for a live album, and I knew how to be a crowd-pleaser. There were only three songs on the *Village Gate* album. That's when we took full advantage of

the capability of what an LP could have on it. People used to say, "Nobody'll play it." But the DJs loved it. They could have coffee, go to the bathroom, and the song would still be playing.

Herbie was being facetious when he made those comments. What he didn't say was that for much of his recording career up until 1961, the jazz albums he made consisted of ten to twelve songs, each lasting three to four minutes. Occasionally, Herbie's albums featured longer songs, but these were aimed at the bebop crowd and were strictly "wailing" sessions. With *Herbie Mann at the Village Gate*, Herbie introduced one aspect of his performances that made him famous: the concept of "groove." Herbie Mann's best works combined three distinct elements: rhythm, melodic invention, and the ability to stretch out a performance to accommodate the momentum generated by the groove of the percussion section. This last aspect would remain a constant, even when Herbie continued changing the musical background.

Three songs were featured on *Herbie Mann at the Village Gate*: Ben Tucker's "Comin' Home Baby" (eight minutes and thirty-seven seconds), and two songs from George and Ira Gershwin's *Porgy and Bess*: a moody "Summertime" (clocking in at ten minutes and eighteen seconds), and a Middle Eastern--flavored version of "It Ain't Necessarily So" (a whopping nineteen minutes and fifty-five seconds, which consumed the entire second side of the LP). The album cover featured a painting by noted Turkish artist Abidin Dino, reflecting the influence of producer Nesuhi Ertegun, who was also from Turkey and an inveterate collector of Surrealist art.

"Comin' Home Baby" was the hit record Herbie had been seeking for nearly a decade. The song begins with an irresistible pulse generated by the two bass players, Ahmed Abdul-Malik and the song's composer, Ben Tucker. The rhythm section played for nearly a minute before Herbie came in to play the melody. For five minutes, his flute danced over the rhythmic background with a melodic, inventive solo before giving way to vibraphonist Hagood Hardy, who hummed along with his own chorus, as was his style. Herbie remembered:

"Comin' Home Baby" was brought to me two days before we recorded the album by Ben Tucker, who was playing with Chris

Connor, the other act at the club. He played it for me and I said, "Man, we should do this tune." So I brought him onstage with Ahmed Abdul-Malik, my bass player, and one played, "boom, boom" and the other played "buh-doo-buh-doom." It became a monster hit and it surprised everybody.

The story of that album was incredible. The place was packed. We were already happening in New York. When the group started, Monte Kay got me thirty-five weeks' work in New York, between the Village Gate, the Half Note, the Village Vanguard, and the Five Spot. I was working all the time, not for a lot of money, but I was working.

The night of the recording was like the apocalypse. Ahmed Abdul-Malik was so nervous that when he drove in from Brooklyn, he drove across the Brooklyn Bridge at twenty-five miles an hour and got a ticket for driving too slowly. When he got off the bridge, he was still shaking, and was now driving down the street at fifteen, so a cop gave him a second ticket. Meanwhile, we started recording, but there was a war that had been festering between Chief Bey and Ray Mantilla about who was playing too long and they ended up fighting backstage.

Ray Mantilla recalled that night:

Chief Bey was older than the rest of us. His way was the African way, and my way was the Latino way from the Bronx. Two different things. I was more refined with my drums, but he used these huge drums with six skins and all these deep tones. His drums were weird. And he was doing that African style but couldn't even play a Latin conga beat. That's why Herbie hired us, because he wanted different variations. Everybody had a different way of playing, especially the drummers. It was a battle of the drums, every time we played.

I remember rehearsing the song backstage. We had never played it before, and the next thing we know, we're onstage playing the damn thing. "Comin' Home Baby" was a groove record. Stone-cold groove. Nobody was trying to play a lot. That's all we did. We just played our time and put our soul into it.

Herbie Mann at the Village Gate made it to No. 30 on *Billboard*'s top-selling album chart, an incredible feat for a jazz album. It stayed on the charts for a remarkable forty-one weeks. To help stimulate radio airplay, Atlantic issued an edited single version (which included part of Herbie's solo and part of Ben Tucker's bass solo) that ran two minutes and thirty-three seconds to accommodate Top 40 stations whose formats did not permit the playing of the entire eight-and-a-half-minute track. It was a pattern the pop-minded Atlantic continued for the duration of Herbie's stay with the label.

For the first time since the big-band era, jazz records were getting airplay on mainstream radio stations. Songs like Cannonball Adderley's "African Waltz," Vince Guaraldi's "Cast Your Fate to the Wind," and Jimmy Smith's "Walk on the Wild Side" were all 45 rpm single hits in the early 1960s.

Enough material was recorded that night at the Village Gate to accommodate a second LP, issued in 1962. *Herbie Mann Returns to the Village Gate* contained two extended songs from the date: Milt Jackson's "Bags' Groove" (a song Herbie had recorded with Mat Mathews at his first recording session), and "New York Is a Jungle Festival," which featured a feverish drum battle between Ray Mantilla and Chief Bey. The other three songs on the album were recorded in April 1961 and featured Herbie playing a succession of native flutes from his collection: a Peruvian flute on "Candle Dance," the Japanese cane flute on "Bedouin," and on "Ekunda," the flute he played on "Evolution of Mann." "Bedouin" and "Ekunda" were both from Herbie's "African Suite." (The album's cover art was another abstract painting by Abidin Dino.)

The huge success of *Herbie Mann at the Village Gate* took *DownBeat* by surprise. Jazz albums did not have a habit of crossing over to the pop charts. Reviewer Harvey Pekar didn't know whether to call the album jazz or heterogeneous ethnic music, and dismissed Herbie's inventive solo on "Comin' Home Baby" as merely "a series of clichés." But there was little doubt that Herbie had broken through the bebop barrier of the 1950s and was now emerging as a crossover favorite.

In December, Herbie held a recording session with the Bill Evans Trio that resulted in the album called *Nirvana*. (The session would conclude with an additional date the following May.) Herbie was understandably nervous to be playing with someone he considered one of his musical heroes.

> I was getting a little frustrated because I thought I was being perceived as a one-dimensional player. Excitement and groove—that's all I was good for. Bill Evans was at the other end of the spectrum. He was sensitive and quiet. But I loved his music, and since Monte Kay was managing him too, he arranged for us to do the *Nirvana* album. I was totally intimidated, playing with a hero, and I was embarrassed by my playing.
>
> One year at Newport, John Coltrane came over to me and said, "You know, I think you insulted my religion when you called the album *Nirvana*." I said, "We're not talking about any religion." I really wanted to call the album *Water Lilies*, but we couldn't get permission from the Monet estate to use the painting as a cover. So Nesuhi Ertegun came up with the idea of "nirvana," which means "peace and tranquility." So Coltrane accepted that, and then he said a funny thing to me. He said, "You know, I'm jealous of you." I said, "*You're* jealous of *me*? Please explain this one." He said, "You can do whatever you want and I'm typecast. I'm 'the avant-garde jazz saxophonist.' You can play with strings, Latin, Brazilian, Bill Evans, whatever you want. I wish I could do that."

In later years, Herbie vowed someday to make up for what he perceived as his poor performance on *Nirvana*. He would do so, but not for another thirty years, by which time Bill Evans had long since passed away.

All during this period, Herbie's mind was still occupied by the sensuous, pulsating sounds he had heard in Brazil that summer. In 1962, he would finally return to Rio, armed with fiscal leverage due to the success of the *Village Gate* album, which helped him convince Atlantic to allow him to record there. He couldn't wait to go.

15

BOSSA NOVA FEVER

Not long after the *Village Gate* album, Herbie made a change in his band's sound, cutting in half the number of men in the rhythm section. Rudy Collins departed to play for Dizzy Gillespie, Chief Bey took his drums back to Africa, and Ahmed Abdul-Malik embarked on his own Middle Eastern musical projects. Herbie redesigned his new band to conform to the softer, more melodic sounds of bossa nova. "The African thing, as a special thing in itself, is all over," he told *DownBeat* with a degree of finality. Herbie soon realized that excitement was not enough for him. Although the percussion showcases dazzled audiences and critics alike, they left him in the background. It wasn't until he went to Brazil that he realized the beauty his flute could bring to the mix.

After the reorganization in January 1962, his percussion section was reduced to Patato Valdes on congas and Willie Bobo on drums. Herbie explained to *DownBeat* his frustration with having so many drummers in his band, each with a different ethnic influence. "The first thing you have to know is that drummers are very narrow-minded," he said. "That is the basic trouble with drums. It is tough for drummers to think some other way." Herbie pointed out that each drummer had his own style, which was unmusical and devoted to a particular cultural heritage: Olatunji and Chief Bey to Africa, Ray Mantilla to salsa and Ray Barretto to jazz.

In an open letter to *DownBeat*, Barretto, who had played in Herbie's band from January until May 1961, took issue with this, defending the "narrow-minded" drummers and explaining that all of them were thorough professionals who listened musically as well as rhythmically:

Almost all the drummers listed quit the band at one time or another. As a guiding force, as a source from which to draw enthusiasm, this Herbie Mann never got across to the fellows. Thus, the excitement that "got away" from him.

Another change that Herbie made in his band was to reintroduce the guitar as a secondary lead instrument. The idea came to him after hearing Brazilian guitarist Baden Powell during his 1961 visit to Rio. Upon arriving back in New York, Herbie hired West Coast sideman Billy Bean to play guitar, returning to the flute/guitar dynamic with which he'd started his career.

Bossa nova wasn't the only new music Herbie was listening to. Ray Charles's recent Atlantic hit "What'd I Say" featured an electric piano, which influenced Herbie to have vibraphonist Hagood Hardy play the instrument on some of Herbie's own R&B-flavored compositions. Herbie was always fascinated with new instruments and had purchased an electric piano of his own back in 1957, mainly to facilitate composing and arranging without disturbing Ruth, plugging in his headphones and working peacefully while she watched television. He also figured out how to play records through the device.

On his next album, *Right Now*, Herbie wrote two songs spotlighting the R&B sound of Hardy's electric piano, combining it with the new dance craze, the Twist, on the funky title track (which Atlantic issued as a single) and highlighting Afro-Cuban rhythms on "Free for All." In the notes to the album, Herbie explained that his band was "like a Monet painting in that the colors overlap and splash so that when you get real close, nothing seems too definite. But then, when you step back, you see the component parts and the whole thing gives you a response."

Right Now was one of two albums in which Herbie first demonstrated his mastery of bossa nova. According to Herbie, bossa nova was simply a "modern and more lyrical version of the samba," championed by young Rio beachgoers. "When they dance to it, they act very cool, not at all the way they do when they dance in their Carnival style. The big difference between the way they play it down there and the way we play it is that they play it straight and we improvise. That's why it's jazz."

Four songs on *Right Now* were the creation of bossa nova composers Antônio Carlos Jobim and Luis Bonfá, including the famous theme from *Black Orpheus*, "Manhá de Carnaval," which Herbie played not as a wistful lament, but with a churning *batucada* background underneath the melody. Herbie understood that the essence of Brazilian music must include its rhythms as well as the melodies, and his recording, retitled "Carnival," had that intoxicating Brazilian flavor he was looking for.

The album cover featured Herbie in a now familiar off-kilter pose, bent backward at the waist in a stance Willis Conover described in his notes to the *Village Gate* album as a "half-hula." Herbie was also now coming out of his shell as a performer. The excitement of the Afro-Cuban experience made him a more sensual performer, and with the intoxicating melodies of the Brazilian songs he was now playing, Herbie became a sexual magnet. The audiences for bossa nova were basically young men and women in their twenties, and the thirtysomething Herbie, with his receding hairline and Mitch Miller beard, became irresistible to women through his sensuous performing style. Dave Pike, who replaced Hagood Hardy on vibraphone, recalled:

> His act became very visual. He got people to play for him who could excite the audience. Herbie would gyrate his body to take people's minds off his playing. He did this to compensate because he was not much of a musician. I'm sorry to say this because I loved the guy, but to some of the musicians he was a laughingstock. Nobody really took him seriously except the record companies and his audiences. But we worked constantly. We worked more in Manhattan than any other band. We played everywhere in Manhattan, and sometimes, we wouldn't even leave town. And he had a good manager, Monte Kay, who also managed the Modern Jazz Quartet. His connections were immense, so he got Herbie all over the world.

A second bossa nova--oriented album that came out in 1962 used the same band, but was recorded for United Artists' jazz series. Herbie explained:

I had a special deal with Atlantic because they never gave me the money I wanted, so they gave me the right to do one album during a three-year contract for another label. What I would do is use that to test the waters and see if that other label could do better than Atlantic. The only problem with that concept—and I'm thinking I'm very clever as a businessperson—is that you can't just do a one-shot for anybody. You have to build on previous releases and it takes time. But they gave me that freedom.

The album was called *Brazil, Bossa Nova & Blues*, and unlike *Right Now*, it featured exclusively Brazilian-flavored music. *DownBeat* called the propulsive rhythm section of Willie Bobo and Patato Valdes "irresistible, yet with restraint." Herbie had learned to ride the waves of the percussionists without being obscured by them, as he often was during his Afro-Cuban period. In addition to first-ever recordings of "One Note Samba" and "Minha Saudade," Herbie wrote two numbers, the driving "B. N. Blues" ("B. N." for "bossa nova"), which he played on a native flute, and "Copacabana," a masterpiece of understated beauty played in a minor key in the low register of the alto flute, with Bobo and Valdes motoring along in the background like a well-tuned car engine in low gear.

Although Herbie Mann was at the forefront of the bossa nova infusion into American jazz, he wasn't alone. Spearheading the attack were tenor saxophonist Stan Getz and guitarist Charlie Byrd, both of whom had also become enamored with bossa nova. In February 1962, one month prior to Herbie's sessions for Atlantic and United Artists, Getz and Byrd recorded *Jazz Samba* for Verve Records. Released in April, the album became a huge hit, stimulating a tidal wave of interest in bossa nova that lasted for two years. By early 1963, it actually topped *Billboard*'s "Top LPs" chart, the first jazz album ever to reach that lofty position. It remained a best seller for most of that year, spending an unprecedented seventy weeks on the charts.

Herbie watched this phenomenon helplessly, irked that he was among the first to be on the scene when he went to Brazil with the Monte Kay tour the previous summer. But Atlantic was hamstrung, preoccupied with the *Village Gate* album and unable to follow it up until it had run its course. Although *Village Gate*, which was released in May, was a hit, *Jazz Samba* sold much better. It's ironic that because *Village Gate* was such a success, Atlantic had to delay the release of *Right Now*, which contained Herbie's first explorations into bossa nova, until September. The United Artists album wasn't issued until after *Jazz Samba* reached No. 1 on the charts in the spring of 1963, so although Herbie and Getz/Byrd recorded their initial forays into bossa nova within a few weeks of each other, Getz/Byrd got to the marketplace first and received the recognition Herbie so desperately desired. It was a tough blow for Herbie, who had spent a decade working to make himself attractive to crossover, mainstream audiences.

When I came back from Brazil, I was working at Basin Street East where Stan Getz was also performing. So I said to him, "I hear you did a bossa nova album." He said, "No, no, it's jazz samba." Well, I had already started playing bossa nova in my act. The Stan Getz/Charlie Byrd album caused quite a stir because it was something brand new to the American audience. But I was playing bossa nova more than Stan Getz was—and doing it live. I tried to talk Atlantic into going down to Brazil, because I didn't think that was the way Brazilian music should sound.

One day, I was walking down Fifth Avenue and I saw a building with a Brazilian flag in front. I stormed inside, and before the person behind the counter could say anything, I said, "Can I speak to the person in charge? I'm a musician. My name is Herbie Mann, and I LOVE Charlie Byrd, and I LOVE Stan Getz, but their music has NOTHING to do with Brazil. Is that the kind of record you want to show what Brazilian music is about?" The guy starts laughing and says, "This is the Economic Council. But let me get on the phone." He called the cultural attaché, got an appointment, and by the time I got through, I had two first-class tickets on Varig, talked Atlantic into it—Nesuhi Ertegun flew down with me—we went to Brazil, held court every night at the Copacabana Palace, and the musicians came and played their music for me. I picked the tunes, picked the musicians, and we did the album.

Unlike Getz/Byrd, whose band consisted of a sextet of American jazz musicians, Herbie Mann used exclusively Brazilian musicians in his four-day session, including the cream of the Rio nightclub scene: the Baden Powell Group, the Sérgio Mendes Bossa Nova Rio Group, the Luís Carlos Vinhas Trio, vocalist João Gilberto, bossa nova paterfamilias Antônio Carlos Jobim, and even a contingent from Brazil's "School of Samba," a group of seventeen young percussionists called Zezinho e Sua Escola de Samba. Herbie recalled:

> Sérgio had a bebop band. His band was an Art Blakey/Horace Silver band with a samba beat. He had a trumpet, a trombone, Paulo Moura on alto sax; Dom Um Romão was the drummer. So the tunes that I did with Sérgio were just Sérgio's regular repertoire that I added myself to. I think that afterwards, a lot of those tunes Cannonball and Nat Adderley did with Sérgio's rhythm section in L.A.
>
> Jobim was the main guy for the music. Bossa nova had just started and it was barely coming here, but I was the first to go down there and record with Brazilians. Jobim was writing arrangements for me, and one day I said to him, "Tom, we're doing 'One Note Samba.' You should sing it." He said, "I'm not a singer." I said, "In America, Hoagy Carmichael's not a singer, Johnny Mercer's not a singer. But they sing their music." "Really?" he said. "And you should do it in English," I said. "Really!" he said. He had been writing a tune for me, and he stopped writing and spent the rest of the time just practicing singing in English. So the first song Jobim ever sang was on my album. The tune he stopped writing turned out to be "The Girl from Ipanema," which he ended up giving to Stan Getz!

By the time Herbie Mann got to Brazil in October, *Jazz Samba* was already a monster hit, resulting in a flurry of stories in the trades about the new bossa nova craze. Verve took out a full-page ad in *DownBeat* that asked "What Is Bossa Nova?" and proceeded to explain how their brand of bossa nova wasn't "merely swinging music played over a vague samba rhythm." Getz had already recorded a follow-up album, *Big Band Bossa Nova*, and vibraphonist Cal Tjader issued his own LP, *Cal Tjader Plays the Contemporary Music of Mexico and Brazil.*

When Herbie returned from his recording session in Brazil, he was livid to find the jazz market saturated with what he called "ersatz bossa nova," and attacked the authenticity of the records being made by American jazz artists. "The closest most of them come to it is some kind of samba rhythm, and that isn't really the same thing," he told *DownBeat* in November. "And if you know your rhythms, you have noticed how far away some of the musicians stray: calypso, rhumba, almost anything." Indignant, he continued: "In Brazil, we recorded with the musicians who really play the bossa nova. I played with the people who can really play it, and I used everyone I could find, varying them from track to track. It will surprise some people and make some others feel pretty silly."

The debate about what constituted bossa nova continued through the winter of 1962/63. In December Herbie told *DownBeat* that although Brazilian musicians were "bugged because we aren't playing it authentically," he was now allowing this kind of latitude because, as he pointed out, the same thing was occurring in Brazil. "It seems as if it had all begun there when João Gilberto, a guitarist, used it as an accompaniment for a singer. Then the drummers picked it up. The audience for it was young and very hip. Part of the reason for that is that it isn't just a rhythm. It's also the implied rhythm. It's also the mood." Herbie said that if it wasn't for Americans appropriating the style, bossa nova would already be on the wane in Brazil:

> One of the most important things about bossa nova is that it should be simple. The Brazilians use that word as a real compliment. Simple and real. Most Brazilians, however, weren't interested in that; they wanted more to hear the old samba. So, about four months ago, most of the musicians playing bossa nova were ready to give up. It seemed to be dying in Brazil. Instead, with the impetus from here, it's achieving a new popularity, though it's still restricted to a small audience.

In March 1963, Herbie's Brazilian album finally came out, nearly a year after the release of *Jazz Samba*. *Do the Bossa Nova* was given an enthusiastic rave by *DownBeat*'s John A. Tynan, who said, "Lest there be any doubt still hanging around about what bossa nova is and how it relates to jazz, this set should quickly put them to flight. It is just about as definitive as possible, and with Mann playing inspired jazz flute, its creative quality is excellent."

The album revealed the entire spectrum of Brazilian jazz, not just the newer bossa nova sound. In addition to Jobim's vocal debut on "One Note Samba," the album featured such highlights as Sérgio Mendes's exuberant version of Clifford Brown's "Blues Walk" and Baden Powell's exquisite "Consolacao," with Herbie playing off of Powell's lyrical guitar with his alto flute. Closing the album was the celebratory "Bossa Velha," which featured the School of Samba's seventeen percussionists, joyously playing a veritable museum of traditional rhythm instruments, including the *cuica, tamborim, reco reco, pandeiro, frigideira, surdo,* and *chocalho. Do the Bossa Nova* proved to be one of the finest albums Herbie Mann ever recorded: authentic, varied in its sounds and influences, exciting, sentimental, rhythmically potent, and infectiously inventive.

But it came too late. By the time the album Herbie had moved mountains to make was released, it was just another in a tsunami of bossa nova--themed albums flooding record stores. By the end of 1963, the craze had burned itself out, as a new musical wave invaded America: the rock 'n' roll British Invasion spearheaded by the Beatles, which snuffed out bossa nova like a candle in a soft, hot Rio wind.

By that time, Herbie had moved on to other musical landscapes, and even begun thinking about how to latch onto the massive success of the Beatles. As for bossa nova, the credit for bringing the music to the United States went to Stan Getz, and years after it happened, the thought still rankled Herbie. In later years, he grew philosophical about the turn of events, but remained steadfast.

> Everybody says that Stan started the craze. I'd say that he was responsible for part of it. But when I went down to Brazil in the mid-nineties for the first time since '64, I'd get notes backstage saying, "We know it was you."

16

OPENING THE DOOR

Herbie Mann was too busy with live concerts during 1963 to make records. That year, he only held one session, cutting four songs that appeared on his *Latin Fever* album. The remaining tracks on the LP were leftovers from his Rio session, songs featuring Antônio Carlos Jobim, Sérgio Mendes, and Baden Powell.

In July, Atlantic recorded Herbie's third appearance at the Newport Jazz Festival, with portions issued on the album *Herbie Mann Live at Newport*. The record showed him in the full flowering of his bossa nova period. Dave Pike, who replaced Hagood Hardy on vibraphone, was with Herbie from 1961 to 1965. Like Hardy, Pike hummed along with his improvisations when he played. He cited Paul Bley, Bud Powell, and Oscar Peterson as inspirations for this technique. The guitarist role so important to Brazilian music was now filled by Attila Zoller. Herbie recalled:

> The band wasn't really a bossa nova band, but Attila, being Hungarian, was one of the few non-Brazilians that could play bossa nova. I played him Baden Powell records and he learned how to comp. So he was the only one I ever heard who wasn't Brazilian who could play that way.

Pike recalled Zoller coming to the band:

> Billy Bean, who played guitar with Herbie, was an alcoholic. I

remember he knocked my vibes off the Village Gate stage once, about six feet, in the dark. He was not reliable, so Herbie got Attila Zoller. Attila came from a little town in Hungary and then moved to Vienna. When he got there, he forgot how to speak Hungarian and never really learned to speak German well either. Then he went from Vienna to Berlin and still couldn't speak either language. He really couldn't speak anything. So when he came to the States, I was assigned to take care of him and I would drive him around. We became good friends. Attila was an interesting guy. And he was a giant of a man, too. I remember one time we were in an airport checking in, and Attila wanted to take his amp with him on the plane. His amp was a Gibson with tubes, and it had to weigh at least a hundred pounds. So the guy asked him if he had any hand luggage, and Attila picks up the amp by the handle and raises it as high as his shoulders and says, "Nah, just this."

Willis Conover noted that Herbie treated the bossa nova standard "Desafinado" as a straight-ahead 4/4 jazz number in his "Latin Manhattan" style. Herbie was already softening his emphasis on the overexposed bossa nova style. Herbie later said:

> Everybody did it. Everybody was doing everything. Everybody recorded "The Girl from Ipanema," "Desafinado," "One Note Samba." That became the new repertoire. It wasn't Charlie Parker anymore. The crossover repertoire then was the bossa nova.

Characteristically, Herbie was getting restless and wanted to move on. He finished first for the seventh consecutive year as the most popular jazz flutist in the *DownBeat* Readers Poll, collecting more than twice as many votes as his closest challenger, Yusef Lateef.

In September, Herbie and Ruth adopted another child, naming this one Claudia, who recalled:

> My dad got a call from some DJ who said, "I've got this kid. She has blonde hair and blue eyes. You have twenty-four hours to come and get her if you want her." The only thing I knew about my birth

mother—and I don't know how Dad found out—was that she was Italian and already had other kids. But I got to thinking that maybe I was Herbie's kid with this woman because later on, I found out too many coincidences. One major one was that my dad, his sister, my sister Laura, and I all have the same tooth on the bottom row that is bent backwards. It's the exact same tooth.

Paul and I had a nanny and a maid and we never wanted for anything. He was an all-right dad. When he was with me, he gave me his time. I was a troublemaker, though, and he would hear about it from my mother and she would start yelling at him. I caused a big rift between them. When I was four, they had a huge blowout fight. They sent me to a boarding school in Brewster, New York, and to Richfield, Connecticut.

They did not have a good marriage. My mother was an alcoholic for a very long time and couldn't handle having two kids. My mother was very smart and very quick, but she was also very hostile. She thought that since she got my father his first break that he owed her something. But he was always away and she just couldn't handle it.

In April 1964, Herbie recorded one of his best bossa nova tracks, "Morning After Carnival," which he played on bass flute, backed by a mesmerizing Middle Eastern--flavored percussion groove provided by Zoller on guitar, Patato Valdes on conga drums, Willie Bobo on timbales, Jack Six on bass, and Bobby Thomas on tambourine.

By the next month, Herbie had basically abandoned bossa nova, reverting back to playing with large orchestras. On *My Kinda Groove*, he teamed up with an orchestra led by Oliver Nelson, mixing styles but staying close to Latin jazz. As always, he kept tabs on what Americans were listening to—and in 1964, America was listening to the Beatles. Spearheading the British Invasion, the talented quartet from Liverpool in turn influenced the burgeoning folk-rock movement, which mutated from the urban folk boom that was starting to lose strength. Starting around the time the bossa nova fad was fading, Herbie decided to make a stronger effort to cater to pop audiences. It marked the first rift between him and jazz critics. To them, Herbie was alienating his base by condescending to "mere" pop audiences. Herbie explained why he went in that direction:

All I ever thought was: Why limit your audience to the fanatics? You're always going to get people that love Charlie Parker, Dizzy Gillespie, and bebop. But that's only five percent of the music-listening audience. I always thought that there's a fringe that loves all other music forms that might want to see something more done with them. So if I play a Ray Charles tune or if I play a Latin tune, or if I play a Crosby, Stills & Nash tune, maybe I'll get some of that audience. So why limit yourself to what your peers say is the only audience that counts? Why not open the door and let everybody else in? I can understand protectionism. I can understand feeling that if too many people like what you consider "good music," that must mean that the music isn't "good" anymore. It's like parity in sports. They're saying that if a lot of people like something, somewhere it lowers the quality, because a lot of people aren't as intelligent as you perceive you are because of the music that you like. But I made that choice, right then and there.

Herbie's new change in direction took effect around 1965, when he started recording tunes from current Broadway hits, popular motion picture themes, and songs from the pop charts. It wouldn't be the last time he would depart from familiar jazz territory, but for the time being, the critics grudgingly acknowledged his doing so. They wouldn't be so kind in later years.

The first inkling of Herbie's new approach was when he devoted an entire album to the score for the Leslie Bricusse/Anthony Newley hit Broadway musical *The Roar of the Greasepaint -- The Smell of the Crowd*. Herbie explained his rationale:

Shelly Manne and André Previn did *My Fair Lady*, and I think certain jazz players were looking for material to improvise on that would broaden the appeal and open the door and invite the non-jazz audience in. It's a decision a lot of people made. Do you want to play small clubs your whole life? Or do you want to attract a bigger audience? I decided I wanted to attract a bigger audience.

Herbie was now back to where he started, playing with a light, swinging sound, except his band was now playing backgrounds more conducive to popular audiences' tastes, much of it infused with the Latin feel that by that point typified Herbie's records (featuring the now ubiquitous Patato Valdes on conga drums). Gone were the eight-minute grooves and lengthy nightclub-oriented improvisations. Herbie's records were now compact, tightly arranged, and concise. Song lengths were cut back to 45 rpm single capacity (two to three minutes). Arranger Ray Ellis provided a full studio orchestra to back Herbie's band, which now included a young twenty-three-year-old pianist named Chick Corea and guitarist Mundell Lowe, who had played with Mat Mathews's group on Herbie's first recordings. Lowe recalled that Herbie had advanced dramatically in the decade since he first recorded with him:

> When I first played with him, I didn't think much of him as a flute player, although he worked on some of my projects. But as I moved out to the coast, I began listening to his records and I realized that he'd grown into a wonderful musician. I was very delightfully surprised. Herbie knew where he was going. It was just a matter of getting there.

Also joining the group in 1965 was drummer Bruno Carr, who would stay with Herbie until the end of 1969. Dave Pike said:

> Bruno Carr was a workhorse. He was a very big guy, but never made waves and never complained about anything. He played well and never got in anybody's way. I could never say that he was particularly exceptional, but he fit the bill.

Herbie's state of mind at that time was amplified in a *DownBeat* interview, which showed that not only was he financially successful, but he also cast a jaded eye at some favorite targets, including agents ("They're incompetent"), jazz critics ("God forbid you should be successful"), Californians ("I find the whole way they live out there unreal"), and American audiences in general ("Most of the people are bores"). By now, he was being viewed as a sex symbol, furthered by the sensuous Latin rhythms he was playing at every show. Women were flocking to him, and his shaky marriage to Ruth wasn't helping him resist their advances. "Some chicks just come in to see me move," he bragged to *DownBeat*. It was the beginning of an arrogance he developed as a defense mechanism because of the jazz community's growing antipathy toward him. Musically, Herbie thought he should be free to play whatever he wanted, but the question critics kept bringing up was whether he was still an "authentic" jazz artist or "selling out."

The Atlantic recording sessions started increasing in frequency. There were no themed albums between 1964 and 1966, just a succession of twelve-song, pop-oriented LPs using disjointed selections from various sessions. *Our Mann Flute* featured a bizarre array of tunes ranging from movie themes like those of *Our Man Flint* and *Malamondo* to covers of the Rascals' "Good Lovin'" and the Mamas and the Papas' "Monday, Monday." There were even two traditional children's songs thrown into the mix, "Skip to My Lou" and "Frère Jacques," and just for good measure, a reissue of a track from *The Common Ground* called "High Life," retitled "Happy Brass," to capitalize on the sensational popularity of the ersatz mariachi music of another Herbie: Herb Alpert and the Tijuana Brass. In addition to being one of the pioneers of the bossa nova craze, Herbie also anticipated the vaunted TJB sound before even Alpert had done so. Alpert's watered-down but accessible version of Mexican mariachi music bore a distinct similarity to the brass-oriented African high-life sound Herbie had been playing on *The Common Ground*. To capitalize on the TJB's fame, "Happy Brass" was reissued as a single, backed by the love theme from the film *Is Paris Burning?*

On the album *Today*, Herbie again presented a mix of contemporary musical themes, including two songs each by Duke Ellington and the Beatles' John Lennon and Paul McCartney. Herbie was an enthusiastic fan of the Beatles' music and covered many of their songs in the ensuing years, showing the universality of the Beatles' excellence by displaying their songs in exotic musical settings. In the album notes, Herbie accurately gauged the importance of the Beatles' rapidly expanding talents, even predicting the massive success of McCartney's ballad "Yesterday."

I feel I can improvise on current pop music as well as early Duke Ellington, and make them both equally valid today. Take the Beatles, for instance. John Lennon and Paul McCartney happen to be two of the most interesting writers on the current scene. The fact that they sell millions of albums to supposedly unsophisticated youngsters doesn't take away from the value of their music. Although the Lennon-McCartney lyrics are important now, it's their music that will last. "Yesterday" should become as much of a standard as Jerome Kern's "Yesterdays." The same goes for Burt Bacharach and Hal David.

On June 1 and 2, 1965, Herbie exercised his unique contract agreement with Atlantic to make an album for Columbia Records. *Latin Mann* featured Herbie's regular group (now including Chick Corea), augmented by Oliver Nelson's big band. The album's central theme was the "Latin jazz family tree." A detailed diagram of the tree, drawn by Herbie, was displayed on the album jacket, showing how the songs influenced jazz in Africa, Spain, and Portugal by way of Cuba, Puerto Rico, and Brazil. Tunes included Horace Silver's 6/8-time hit "Señor Blues," Herbie Hancock's "Watermelon Man" (which had been popularized by Mongo Santamaría), and Nat Adderley's "Jive Samba," all popular 1960s jazz hits with Latin flavoring. Herbie also included Ray Charles's "What'd I Say," whose pulse he labeled as "boom-chitty." "What Afro-Cuban was to Latin jazz, that's what boom-chitty is to rhythm-and-blues," he explained in the notes.

Herbie saved two Afro-Cuban songs for last, the Cuban standard "Ave Maria Morena" and Esy Morales's "Jungle Fantasy." Both were recorded three weeks later with an all-Latin combo consisting of Charlie Palmieri on piano, Bobby Rodriguez on bass, and a percussion section of Rafael Da Vila, Carlos Diaz, and Raymond Sardinis.

By the mid-1960s, Herbie had done more to further the exploration of music in Africa and Latin American than any artist except Dizzy Gillespie. But in 1966 he turned his attention to a region that was quickly becoming one of the world's political hot spots: the Middle East.

17

THE WAILING DERVISHES

In 1966, the world's attention was focused on two regions facing increasing military and political conflict: Vietnam and the Middle East. America was in the process of escalating the number of its troops in South Vietnam to over 385,000. In the Middle East, tensions between Israel and Palestinian militant forces were increasing in severity, which would result in the Six-Day War between Israel and the Arab nations of Syria, Jordan, and Egypt the following June.

In America, Herbie Mann decided he'd had his fill of Brazilian music for a while and was anxious to move on to other horizons.

> We had reached that point where everybody and his brother were playing the bossa nova. So I thought it was time for me to take a break. Looking to where the flute was in ethnic music, the Middle East was an obvious choice for me. I added an oud player, Chick Ganimian, to my band, and we started looking into Middle Eastern music. The oud was the ancestor of the lute. When the French went on the Crusades, they saw the instrument and called it "l'oud," which eventually became "lute." It's a guitarlike instrument with a rounded back.

Herbie was assisted in his efforts by Arif Mardin, a young arranger employed at Atlantic. Like Nesuhi Ertegun, Mardin was born in Istanbul, Turkey, and was delighted when Herbie asked him to recommend traditional Turkish tunes and write arrangements for several of the tracks on the album. In 2000, Mardin recalled:

> Herbie was actually a force at Atlantic. When I first joined Atlantic in 1963, he was making jazz records with Nesuhi Ertegun, who was my boss at that time. Nesuhi had many visions for Herbie, and Herbie was the co-creator of these visions. These were very original aspects at that time, but that was Herbie's style. I liked to experiment and he did, too. I was a graduate of the Berklee College of Music, but I was just doing basically clerical work at Atlantic when I first joined them. So it was Herbie who sought me out and asked me if I could do these arrangements for his album. Herbie and King Curtis were both very helpful to me during the beginning of my career at Atlantic. Herbie recorded one of my songs called "The Young Turks," which he recorded on *Monday Night at the Village Gate*, so he asked me for some recommendations.

Mardin contributed four arrangements to *Impressions of the Middle East*. There were two traditional Turkish folk songs, "Uskudar" and "Yavuz," and one of his own compositions, "Odalisque." In addition, he responded to Herbie's desire to record current pop songs by crafting an arrangement of Manfred Mann's "Do Wah Diddy Diddy," by the Brill Building team of Jeff Barry and Ellie Greenwich.

Herbie wrote four songs of his own for the album, the infectious "Turkish Coffee," the mystical, Islamic-flavored "Incense" (named for the sticks of incense burning in the studio during the session), a bluesy arabesque Herbie whimsically titled "The Oud and the Pussycat," and the up-tempo, spirited "Dance of the Semites."

The album featured the debut of Herbie's new vibraphonist, Roy Ayers, who replaced Dave Pike in the band. Just twenty-five, Ayers was a product of South Central Los Angeles, which had recently been engulfed in the Watts race riots that occurred the previous summer. Ayers grew up listening to R&B, but eventually switched to jazz after hearing the Modern Jazz Quartet's Milt Jackson and Ayers's idol, Lionel Hampton. Herbie recalled hiring Ayers in California:

I was playing a gig at the Lighthouse in Hermosa Beach, and I had a trombone player named Jack Hitchcock who also doubled on vibes. Roy came in one night, looking for the job. He asked to sit in, he played, and I hired him. He is an incredible vibraphonist. I produced his first records. Finally, I pushed him out of the band after about eight or nine years because I told him he should be a leader. I like the combination of flute and vibes because there are less chord notes played, so there's more space.

Herbie's group recorded during three dates in March and one in November before finally completing the album, which was released in early 1967. Herbie was also working on an album featuring a twenty-one-piece string ensemble conducted by Torrie Zito, but plucked Zito's arrangement of the Jewish dirge "Eli, Eli" from the session to finalize the *Middle East* album.

"Eli, Eli" was a song composer Jacob Koppel Sandler wrote in 1896 for the operetta *The Hero & Bracha*. It was published and made famous ten years later when Yiddish theater star Sophia Karp performed it in another operetta, *Rouchel*. Zito's melancholy arrangement and Herbie's emotional solo provided a disquietingly beautiful footnote to the *Middle East* album.

As innovative as Herbie had been in recording in the Afro-Cuban, Latin, and Brazilian idioms, *Impressions of the Middle East* was the first time a major jazz musician had turned his attention to the musical traditions of the cradle of civilization. It was the ultimate fusion between West and East, the distant past and the turbulent present.

On June 3, 1967, Atlantic recorded a live album at New York's Village Theater, where Herbie and his band were currently appearing. Now at the height of his Middle Eastern experiment, Herbie and his band generated more heat than they bargained for that night, considering the volatile political atmosphere in Israel. Herbie recalled:

That album was recorded on the first night of the Six-Day War. I had three Arabs in the band and a couple of Jews. Backstage, the Arabs were very upset. Before we went on, I went backstage and said, "You know what? Those are politicians; we are musicians. We are here. They are there. If you want to use this as a reason not to play, you can leave right now. I've played without you guys before and I can play without you now. It's your choice." So that was it. They all stayed.

The album cover for *The Wailing Dervishes* featured a psychedelic design by Marvin Israel, a surrealist artist who had recently become the art director at *Mademoiselle* magazine. Instead of the usual liner notes, the back cover displayed a quotation from thirteenth-century Persian poet Jalāl ad-Dīn Rūmī.

The Wailing Dervishes proved to be one of the most exciting albums Herbie ever recorded. True to form, he accented the Middle Eastern musical vernacular by applying it to a current popular song, the Beatles' "Norwegian Wood." (With tongue in cheek, Herbie announced the number as "The Decline and Fall of the British Empire.") The result was a ten-and-a-half-minute extravaganza in 6/8 time that took the song to places even the acid-tripping John Lennon couldn't have imagined, featuring burning-hot solos by Ayers, Ganimian, and then Herbie. Finally, the percussion section took over for a final furious flurry, punctuated by shrieking squeals from Ganimian's oud, which set the audience into a frenzy of cheering.

Herbie took fusion to its outer limits by inviting Scottish bagpipe player Rufus Harley to play his own composition "Flute Bag." The experiment deserved applause for no other reason than the fact that it could be accomplished at all, although jazz on the bagpipes proved to be nothing more than just an oddity.

Herbie Mann's brief foray into Middle Eastern music came during a year when the Beatles, the Rolling Stones, and Jefferson Airplane were the presumptive leaders of the so-called "Summer of Love." There were other worlds outside the U.S. that Herbie was interested in exploring, but as 1968 dawned, he turned inward to explore one of America's own indigenous music styles.

18

THE KENNY G OF THE SIXTIES

Although Middle Eastern music was a major part of Herbie Mann's repertoire during 1966 and 1967, he was still working toward cracking the mainstream pop music market. In addition to releasing *Impressions of the Middle East* and *The Wailing Dervishes*, Atlantic was still mining the last vestiges of the bossa nova craze. In 1967, they repackaged Herbie's 1962 Rio recordings, giving equal billing on the cover to João Gilberto and Antônio Carlos Jobim.

Also issued that year was an album pairing Herbie with singer Tamiko Jones, an exotic-looking singer whose ancestry boasted equal elements of Japanese, British, and Cherokee Indian roots, a mix that no doubt attracted the multiculturally minded Herbie. Mann had heard Jones sing during a rehearsal in Atlantic's New York studios and was taken with the twenty-one-year-old's sensuous pop-oriented voice, which bore a remarkable similarity to that of Dionne Warwick.

The first song they recorded was a cover of the theme from the movie *A Man and a Woman*, which resulted in the obvious titling of the album, *A Mann & A Woman*. The LP was highlighted by three arrangements by pianist Joe Zawinul, then a member of the Cannonball Adderley Quintet and future founder of Weather Report, who sat in with Herbie's group at the session. One of Zawinul's arrangements was a ripping version of the current Lennon & McCartney hit "Day Tripper." Zawinul's soulful piano was put to its best effect on Jones's own composition, "A Good Thing (Is Hard to Come By)." Covers of other contemporary pop songs like Len Barry's "1-2-3" and Bobby Hebb's "Sunny" made it clear Herbie was leaving the jazz repertoire behind in search of crossover material.

More of the same was in store for *The Beat Goes On*, whose title track was a hit for Sonny & Cher, then riding high on the pop charts with their recordings on Atco, an Atlantic subsidiary. Sonny Bono himself produced Herbie's recording of the title track. The rest of the album was described by *DownBeat* as sounding like it was produced on an assembly line, with the exception of Dave Pike's bossa nova--flavored "Dream Garden," which came from a 1964 session. *DownBeat* was becoming less and less patient with Herbie's abilities as a flutist, and despite his surrounding himself with top-notch sidemen, the magazine rarely gave Herbie more than grudging compliments, accusing him of unimaginative, cliché-ridden improvisations and a thin, soulless tone. Reviewer Peter Erskine delivered a veiled threat of further ill treatment by the magazine: "He does not do much more than play melody with simple embellishments, and nothing in this album is going to improve his stature as a jazz musician."

The songs on Herbie's albums were now almost routinely geared for pop radio airplay, rarely more than three minutes in length, allowing for little in the way of extended improvisations, except on the occasional live album. The ultimate attempt at crossing over came with the release of *The Herbie Mann String Album*, which featured the lush Torrie Zito arrangements that had been recorded the previous year. Herbie Mann was now being viewed by jazz critics as a purveyor of pop-tune covers, a handful of original compositions, and film music themes and show tunes. As far as many of them were concerned, Herbie's records would be better suited filed under "Easy Listening" in America's record stores.

Herbie's blatant targeting of the pop charts was obvious and calculated, but Herbie didn't mind explaining to anyone who would listen his reasons for it. Starting in the mid-1960s, the jazz community started resenting the fact that Herbie was abandoning the traditional jazz repertoire to reach mainstream audiences. His popularity among his fans was still strong, reflected by *DownBeat's* annual Readers Poll, which consistently placed him far ahead of other, more conventional jazz flutists. The consortium of jazz critics, however, was just as consistent in putting him toward the middle of the pack, well behind other, "more serious," jazz flute players like Rahsaan Roland Kirk, Yusef Lateef, and Eric Dolphy. Herbie was resigned to this attitude.

> They've always hated me. I was the Kenny G of the sixties, except he was a much better player than I was then. But I was sticking my tongue out at the fact that jazz was Charlie Parker/Dizzy Gillespie/Miles Davis. I was saying, "Jazz is nobody." And they said, "No, jazz is this tradition." And I said, "Well, why don't you just call my music something else, then?" I want to be very musical, but I also want a lot of people to know it. Fortunately, I sold enough records of my hits that Atlantic let me do what I wanted.

In 1967, Herbie exercised the clause in his Atlantic contract that allowed him to record for another label and made an album for A&M Records, the Los Angeles--based powerhouse started by Herb Alpert, creator of the massively popular Tijuana Brass sound, and businessman Jerry Moss. Part of the reason Herbie chose A&M was because the album would be produced by Creed Taylor, an old friend from Herbie's days recording for Bethlehem in the 1950s. Herbie recalled:

> Creed was a visionary. He was the first one to take great jazz players and do pop songs. On all those records, during all those years, his rhythm section was Herbie Hancock, Ron Carter, and Tony Williams doing pop tunes, because he figured that jazz players could do pop tunes better than studio players. Quincy [Jones] does that also. He always gets great jazz players to play the music. And Creed had this vision.

> I was beginning to move toward trying some other things. Ray Charles was a very strong influence, and so was R&B, so I was listening to that music. My musical taste is like a smorgasbord table. I listen to everything and I want to do everything. Look at the record. There was one Brazilian cut, "Upa Neguinho"; there were some things with a small group; we did "Hold On, I'm Comin'" and "Unchain My Heart"; and I did a duet with Hubert Laws.

The A&M album, titled *Glory of Love*, showed Herbie beginning to move into soul music for the first time. The jazz/gospel combination that Charles melded into what was now becoming known as "soul" permeated the album, from the bluesy tones of Herbie's alto flute on "No Use Cryin'" to the joyous church gospel of "Unchain My Heart" and the folk/blues standard "House of the Risin' Sun." The title track, a No. 1 song for Benny Goodman during the big-band era, was a hit for the Dominoes in the 1940s before Ray Charles recorded it for Atlantic. Herbie's version emulated Otis Redding's recent recording for Volt, another Atlantic subsidiary, which started with a slow 6/8 gospel lilt before finishing in 4/4, with Herbie's flute mimicking the Memphis brass riffs on the rideout.

Joining Herbie on the album was a young, classically trained jazz flute player named Hubert Laws. Laws would later assume Herbie's position as the premier jazz flute player, who, like Herbie, focused on the flute as his main instrument, unlike other musicians like Rahsaan Roland Kirk and Yusef Lateef, who were primarily reed players. Characteristically, Herbie never felt threatened by Laws, who was much more accomplished musically, even though he was still only in his twenties. Herbie was always magnanimous in his praise for not only Laws, but also other flute players.

Hubert was the young hotshot flute player in New York, so I asked him if he would play with me. He's probably the best flute player there is. He was classically trained, so he was an excellent reader, had a great sound, and I really loved the way he played. As far as an all-around flute player, I'd say he was the best. He didn't have to learn anything from me. He was perfect already.

A second album for A&M, titled *Trust in Me*, was recorded early in 1968, but because Herbie was only permitted to do one album for each contract period for another label, he wasn't allowed artist credit. Instead, *Trust in Me* was credited to the Soul Flutes, with the unnamed Herbie referred to in the liner notes as "The Fluteman." Like *Glory of Love, Trust in Me* was produced by Creed Taylor, who this time employed Don Sebesky as arranger of the innovative song selection. The stellar supporting cast included Herbie Hancock, Bucky Pizzarelli, Eric Gale, and four studio flute players, who bolstered the Fluteman's work on an ethereal version of Simon & Garfunkel's "Scarborough Fair."

In between recording the A&M albums, Atlantic reunited Herbie with Carmen McRae for a 45 rpm single featuring the theme song from the French motion picture *Live for Life* (starring Yves Montand and a young Candice Bergen), backed by an ancient Tin Pan Alley standard from 1929, "A Cottage for Sale." Despite being advertised heavily in the trades, the record stiffed.

Herbie was now feeling that, with the popularity of Motown and Stax, soul and R&B was a good direction to take his music. Although he was one of the most financially secure musicians in pop music, he had not had a hit record since "Comin' Home Baby" in 1962. Continuing his practice of going to the source to find musicians who played the styles he wanted to explore, Herbie went to the center of soul and R&B's activity: Memphis.

19

MEMPHIS UNDERGROUND

Herbie Mann had been blowing hot and cold with jazz critics ever since he started departing from performing jazz standards and bebop in the 1950s. His experiments in Afro-Cuban and Brazilian music were recognized as exhilarating and exciting, but in embracing pop and rock music numbers like "The Beat Goes On" and "Monday, Monday," he was beginning to alienate jazz mainstays. Jazz critics and fellow musicians had never been as enthusiastic about Herbie's musicianship as had been his fans, but for Herbie, the fans were all that mattered.

In 1968, Herbie made an addition to his band that had a bigger effect on his separation from jazz fans than any other: guitarist Sonny Sharrock. Initially, Sharrock wanted to learn the saxophone, after hearing John Coltrane's work on Miles Davis's seminal *Kind of Blue* album. But asthma prevented him from doing so, though Sharrock always considered himself "a horn player with a really fucked-up axe." The sounds that emanated from Sharrock's electric guitar were like nothing Herbie Mann—or anyone, for that matter—had ever heard before. Up to that point, guitarists in Herbie's bands were either dyed-in-the-wool beboppers, like Mundell Lowe and Joe Puma, or bossa nova devotees, like Baden Powell and Attila Zoller. In Sharrock's hands, the guitar became a malevolent scepter, a weapon, with dissonant shrieks, overamplified distorted wails, and wild feedback his trademarks.

The latest change in Herbie's sound began with the release of *Windows Opened* in 1968. The album marked the recorded debut of Sharrock on guitar and Miroslav Vitouš on bass as members of his band. Herbie's group, with Roy Ayers on vibraphone and Bruno Carr on drums, was now a tight-knit quintet. *Windows Opened* had its share of surprises on it, including a particularly volcanic version of Donovan's "There Is a Mountain," plus renditions of other pop tunes: Tim Hardin's "If I Were a Carpenter" and Jimmy Webb's "By the Time I Get to Phoenix." Herbie stubbornly stuck to his belief that jazz musicians should embrace the popular music of the day, reflecting his intent to cross over to pop and rock audiences. As on *The Wailing Dervishes*, Herbie dispensed with the usual liner notes by including poems by such writers as John Milton, Arthur Hugh Clough, and Percy Bysshe Shelley, each having to do with the album's theme of windows. It was clear that the message Herbie was trying to convey was to "open the windows" of his music so that non-jazz-oriented audiences could come in. He recalled:

> By that time, Miroslav Vitouš and Sonny Sharrock were in the band. Miroslav was this young, twenty-three-year-old Superman on the bass, and Sonny was this avant-garde guitarist. People used to say to me, "What are those two guys doing in your band?" And I said, "Well, what was Coltrane doing in Miles' band?" Miles was a melodist and Coltrane was this "out" saxophone player. You need foils. And besides, they were originals. How many originals are there in the world? Sonny would do his "out" stuff and then he'd pick up his acoustic guitar and do a duet with me on "Scarborough Fair." Miroslav was listening to the Miles records, so he brought in Wayne Shorter tunes like "Footprints," so at that time, the band was trying to emulate Miles. From there, through *Stone Flute* and *Concerto Grosso*, that was my *Kind of Blue* period.

Windows Opened was well received by critics. The album mostly featured solos by Herbie and Roy Ayers, while Sonny Sharrock was mainly used as part of the rhythm section. Only on Ayers's title track did Sharrock come alive, with a brief sequence of startling runs that reflected the experiments in fusion he would become known for in the 1970s. It wasn't until *Memphis Underground* was recorded later that year that Sharrock would come full flower with his avant-garde work on guitar.

Herbie continued his exploration of soul and R&B in May with his next album, *The Inspiration I Feel*, devoted entirely to the music of Ray Charles. The album cover was an abstract painting of Herbie created by Romanian artist Dimitrie Berea. Herbie framed the original work, which hung in his home office. Herbie dispensed with his quintet for this album in favor of a full orchestra and chorus with arrangements by innovative American composer William Fischer, with whom Herbie would collaborate on his landmark *Concerto Grosso in D Blues* several years later. The only other jazz musician on the date was saxophonist David "Fathead" Newman, who spent twelve years playing in Charles's band. He would eventually sign with Herbie and work in his band for another decade.

In the summer of 1967, Herbie and Ruth went to London on vacation. It was while he was there that he had another musical epiphany, similar to when he first saw *Black Orpheus* in 1961.

> I was in England with my first wife and the Stax/Volt tour came to London, with Sam & Dave, Otis Redding, Booker T. & the MGs, and Eddie Floyd. Tom Dowd was there recording it for Stax, and after the concert, we went to this discotheque. While we were there, we were listening to music and this record came on. I said to him, "Tom, listen to that record." He said, "I'll go see what is." He went into the booth and came out with a 45 called "Mercy" by Willie Mitchell on Hi Records. So we went out and bought the record.

Willie Mitchell was the founding father of the Memphis/Stax sound, a trumpet player whose music was popular with white as well as black audiences. Hi Records was founded in 1957 by Joe Cuoghi, but it was Mitchell who established the label's sound and musical direction. Mitchell understood dance music and soon formed smaller versions of big bands that included blasting horns and soul-drenched, handclapping rhythms. He had a minor hit with an instrumental called "20-75," but spent a lot of his time working behind the mixing board. In 1968, his highest-charting record, "Soul Serenade," reached the top ten on *Billboard*'s R&B chart. "Mercy" had a sultry, pounding, slightly distorted sound, with a pulsating rhythm section highlighted by a powerful brass choir, honking tenor sax, and searing electric guitar. Herbie continued his story:

When we were working on the *Glory of Love* album, I had this tune that I brought in to Creed Taylor, and I said, "Here's this great tune I think I could do with Hubert. And he said, "I don't think it has a strong enough melody." So I saved "Memphis Underground" for my own album. [*Laughs*]

The idea of doing the *Memphis Underground* album with a Southern rhythm section came to me because a lot of my crossover attempts at New York R&B didn't work because I was using jazz rhythm sections. So just as I would go to Brazil for Brazilian music, and Latin America for Latin music, I thought, "Why don't I go to the source of this music?" The studios in Memphis are where they recorded Aretha and Otis Redding, so that was natural for them. So we took my band, which was finishing a tour, with Roy Ayers, Larry Coryell, who was in the band at the time, and Sonny Sharrock, and added the Memphis Rhythm Section.

We got down there the first day, and I thought about something that made a lot of sense to me. If you're a stranger, you don't walk into a studio and say, "Here's what I want to play." You walk in and say, "What do *you* think we should play?" So Tom Dowd and the band went across the street to the record store and found a record called "New Orleans" by Gary U.S. Bonds. So we did that tune on the first day. On the second day, I brought in this tune, "Mercy," and I said, "I've got this tune, and I'd like to see if we could get this groove going; I wrote a new melody for it." I played it for them and they started laughing. And they said, "That's us."

Now you talk about serendipity. Turns out that they were the rhythm section for Willie Mitchell. They made up the groove. Willie called it his tune. There was only one different player; otherwise, it was the same band. A million studios in the world with a million rhythm sections. I find a record in London, bring it to Memphis, and it's the same rhythm section.

The groove on "Memphis Underground" was simple and perfect, played by musicians who were used to playing it at nightclubs: Reggie Young, guitar; Bobby Emmons, organ; Bobby Wood, acoustic and electric pianos; Tommy Cogbill or Mike Leech on Fender bass; and Gene

Christman on drums. *Memphis Underground* became the most important record of Herbie Mann's career because it firmly established him as a crossover artist. Although the single version only reached No. 44 on the pop charts, the album, with the full-length seven-minute version of the title track, made it to No. 22. Herbie recalled:

> I did a spot for public housing, with "Memphis Underground" playing in the background, which became a PSA. It was played on every radio station, every black station, all over the country. And it just mushroomed.

Memphis Underground even caught the attention of notorious "gonzo" journalist Hunter S. Thompson, who put the album at number one in his top ten list of favorite LPs of the 1960s, finishing ahead of works by such artists as Bob Dylan, the Rolling Stones, the Grateful Dead, and even Miles Davis's *Sketches of Spain*.

In addition to the hit title track, the album featured cover versions of two Atlantic soul masterpieces, Sam & Dave's "Hold On, I'm Comin'" and Aretha Franklin's "Chain of Fools." On these records, Sonny Sharrock was unleashed. Herbie defended his latest radical musical move:

> I don't tell musicians what to play. If I hire somebody, I have enough confidence that they're going to be creative. But people would run up to the stage, stamp their fists and say, "THAT'S NOT JAZZ!" But Sonny jarred a lot of people. On "Comin' Home, Baby," the rhythm section was playing straight ahead, so it was still for a jazz audience. Here, all of a sudden, we're going after a different audience. A definite black audience. Years later, this young black girl came over to me during a concert and said to me, "Don't tell me you're white." I said, "I've made over a hundred records. Do you think I look black?" She said, "Man, listen to your music!" And I told her, "That just proves that the color of one's skin has nothing to do with their heart and soul." And she shook her head and said, "Man, I always thought you were black."

20

D BLUES

The success of *Memphis Underground* gave Herbie Mann the freedom to expand his business enterprise. In 1968 he formed Five Faces of Music, a production company where he began producing and managing other artists and publishing new music. A new act, which he called "The Music World of Herbie Mann," made its debut at the Village Gate in what Herbie called "a hip version of *The Fred Waring Show*," in which he presented a package of acts he was managing. The showcase had Herbie lead off conducting a big band, followed by a set by his quintet (with Ayers, Sharrock, Vitouš, and Carr), Steve Marcus's Count's Rock Band, and a comedian.

Sonny Sharrock's guitar playing led *DownBeat* to muse that "Sharrock proved again that you can con Edison," noting that a girl a few tables away from the band had her fingers in her ears. Herbie didn't exactly embrace the excessive volume and asked Sharrock and Vitouš about it, to which they replied that this was the way they always played and that "we can't do our thing if it's not this loud." Herbie said:

> Sonny is from Ossining, New York, but I first heard him with Byard Lancaster. Lots of people again say that this doesn't sound like me. Well, if I wanted a band to sound like me completely, I'd do what George Shearing has done and find a bunch of people that play exactly the same way constantly. It seems to me that if you have a band, the leader should know that every musician who joins the

band should make the band sound different, without being worried that you're going to get lost, because it still is your band.

As if Sonny Sharrock's extraterrestrial wails weren't enough to cause some fans to head for the exits, Sharrock's wife, Linda, made appearances on her husband's Vortex LP *Black Woman*, produced by Herbie. Bringing to mind the vocal hysterics of Beatles doppelgänger Yoko Ono, Linda Sharrock left critic Leonard Feather groping for words to describe her singing. "Indescribable tones emanate from the throat of the guitarist's wife," Feather wrote in the *Los Angeles Times*, "ranging from pure-white-sound soprano to wordless black-shriek anguish." Pat Rebillot, who played with Herbie in the early seventies when Sharrock was still in the band, said:

> Sonny was a doll. His personality didn't quite fit with his music, which was really out there, but he was the sweetest guy. I really liked him. He struggled with diabetes during his life and I guess it finally killed him. Fans either loved him or hated him. His music is not something you could be neutral about. I know that some of the band members weren't too crazy about it either.

The fusion between jazz and rock music was beginning, and Herbie was beginning to recognize that rock audiences were not satisfied with just hearing the melodies of their favorite songs; they wanted to hear improvisation, just as jazz musicians improvised. Herbie found that rock audiences were comfortable with his quintet, so long as he gave them a point of reference, just as he had done by adding percussionists to his band and playing Afro-Cuban music in the 1950s. He told *DownBeat*:

> We played a concert outside of Boston with the Byrds, and they went on first, and the audience was loaded with college kids and very relaxed people, and I said, well, this is definitely their audience and then when we got on, I found out that the audience was ours. They wanted to hear us play the songs they grew up with. They wanted us to play our version of "Norwegian Wood," and our version of "Eight Miles High" and "Mellow Yellow." They know it, but they want something more than the melody.

By 1968, Herbie had begun traveling more abroad, performing with and without his regular band. In the early seventies, he played gigs using the band of his old Brooklyn friend Phil Woods, who had moved to France and was getting more and more involved in avant-garde jazz. Woods recalled:

> He used my band for a couple of gigs, back when I had the European Rhythm Machine. Afterward, I asked the guys, "What was the gig like with Herbie?" They said, "Herbie would say, 'We're going to play in B-flat, slow. And then we're going to go into G and we'll make it kind of rock-ish. And then we'll go into G minor and play beboppish.'" But he never called a tune. It was all free improvisation, and it was pretty darned good. He never had a rehearsal. My guys just showed up and they knew what to do.
>
> He was also one of the highest-paying guys in the business. He made a lot of money, but he also shared the bread. That's something that is not too common, these days or any day. No rehearsals, the best hotels, first-class airfare to Europe, which wasn't that high in those days.
>
> Herbie came to Europe every year, so we'd get a chance to hang out. He'd call me and say, "Who have you got? I need a band." I don't think he was carrying a band all of the time; he had Miroslav and Sonny at that time, but occasionally he'd travel as a single and just pick up a rhythm section.

With more freedom than ever before, Herbie embarked on an ambitious project with William Fischer, who had conducted and arranged the orchestra on *The Inspiration I Feel*. Fischer and Herbie produced the ambitious *Concerto Grosso in D Blues* at Teldec Studios in Berlin, West Germany, during a two-day recording session in November 1968, shortly after the quintet appeared at Berlin Jazz Days. The location was used because symphonic musicians overseas were less expensive to hire than their American counterparts. In the LP's liner notes, Herbie said:

> It's as though Bill was my psychiatrist and spent years and years to find out what's in me and then put it down on paper. I wanted a

piece for symphony and jazz group. So you've got to have someone who knows both: jazz and symphony music. That's been the trouble so far; everyone combining jazz and classical music knew just one field. Bill Fischer knows both.

Fischer combined his New Orleans upbringing with his knowledge of contemporary classical composers like Pierre Boulez and Karlheinz Stockhausen to write a densely layered arrangement for the eighty-piece orchestra, whose members were culled from Radio Free Berlin, the RIAS network, and the Berlin Symphonic Orchestra. Herbie recalled:

> I gave the themes to Bill Fischer, who was brought up in New Orleans, and we wrote "Concerto Grosso in D Blues." It was a play on words. The piece was in the key of D. It was part New Orleans and part contemporary music. Miroslav was supposed to go, but being that he had defected from Czechoslovakia, he didn't want to cross over East Berlin to get to West Berlin, so Ron Carter took his place.

Nesuhi Ertegun, who produced the session, said, "There was so much electricity in the studio, you wouldn't believe it." Years later, Herbie downplayed the work. "I would play it differently now," he said, matter-of-factly. "What Bill did was to write the backgrounds according to the personalities of the performers. He wrote a specific one for Sonny, one for Roy, for Ron Carter, and for Bruno Carr. Later on, he wrote a different interlude, which we never recorded. It was all right for what it was."

The work took up an entire side of the LP, which was released in early 1969. The other side included three chamber pieces featuring the quintet; one with a brass ensemble and the others with a double string quartet. Herbie described the brass piece, "Sense of No Return," as something that continually changes keys. "It never stops, it's round. It's not a square piece with four sides." The other two songs represented some of the most evocative and emotional flute playing of Herbie's career. "Wailing Wall" was first intended for Herbie's Middle Eastern band of 1967, while the poignant, warm, and loving "My Little Ones" was dedicated to Herbie's children, Claudia and Paul. At times, Sharrock's guitar sounded like a

Russian balalaika, while Ron Carter's bass had a touch of Andalusian flamenco in it. After listening to the playback of "My Little Ones" in the studio, Herbie smiled and said, "That's the way my children are."

For Herbie, fusion had come full focus. As he explained in the album notes, "I don't want to play a song like a Middle East or African or Arabian song anymore. Everything, the whole world has to be in it."

21

EMBRYO

After the release of *Memphis Underground*, Atlantic issued only one other LP by Herbie Mann in 1969, a live recording of a July concert at Hollywood's Whisky a Go Go, which featured two extended jams, each of which filled up an entire side of the LP. The first was "Ooh Baby," written by Chris Hills and Columbus Baker, two members of a failed New York band called the Free Spirits. The Free Spirits started out as a jazz quintet, but with the arrival of guitarist Larry Coryell, they soon began combining elements of rock into their music, becoming, along with the Electric Flag and Blood, Sweat & Tears, one of the earliest jazz-rock groups. Most of the band members would later become associated with Herbie Mann's own expansion into jazz-rock in the early 1970s. "Ooh Baby" was a fifteen-minute jam dominated by the honking tenor sax of Steve Marcus, another Atlantic jazz artist who recorded for its Vortex label.

The other side, Rufus Thomas's "Philly Dog," was a more conventional Memphis R&B number that featured a typically anarchic guitar solo from Sonny Sharrock. Both songs showed evidence of Herbie's continuing fascination with rock and jazz.

Only one other Atlantic recording was made in 1969, a bizarre two-part single called "It's a Funky Thing — Right On" in which an edited version of Herbie's recording of "Memphis Underground" was overdubbed with dialog and vocals by Milton Miller Smith (aka "Little Milton Swee-Tee") and Charlie Scruggs (aka "Percy"), portraying girl-watchers cruising down a street in Memphis, commenting in "jive" language particular to the period.

Herbie's recording activity for Atlantic was so dormant because he was preparing his debut on his own label, which would be called Embryo. Distributed by Atlantic's R&B subsidiary Cotillion Records, Embryo had its debut announced at the company's annual sales convention in January 1970. Herbie recalled:

> When it came time to renegotiate my contract, they gave me my own label. It was an Atlantic label that I was now running, called Embryo. My negotiations with Atlantic were always very amenable, because they gave me whatever I wanted and let me do whatever I wanted. If I didn't want the label, I probably could have gotten more money for myself, but it allowed me to produce records, which was one of the things I wanted to try and do.

Full-page ads were taken out in the music trades announcing Embryo's debut, whose slogan was "A New Beginning." By the time Embryo wore itself out two years later, Herbie had produced fifteen albums, including four of his own. The record albums' designs were streamlined to feature a blank, white cover with a die-cut gatefold design in the middle. For its initial release, five LPs were released simultaneously, led by Herbie's own experiment into drug-induced psychedelia, *Stone Flute*. Other releases included solo efforts by Herbie's compatriots Attila Zoller, Ron Carter, and Miroslav Vitouš, plus an album by an Ohio-based jazz fusion group called Brute Force. Herbie matter-of-factly explained the concept behind *Stone Flute*: "I just wanted to make a stoned record. Did the whole record under the influence of marijuana."

The album cover featured one of Herbie's ethnic stone flutes set in a sea of rounded pebbles, but the album title's pun failed to disguise the fact that there was definitely a chemical musical influence prevalent on the record. The six moody tracks sounded as if they were being played back at a slower speed, with Herbie using the alto and bass flute much of the time. Eerie drones, echo effects, and reverb permeate "Miss Free Spirit" and "In Tangier/Paradise Beach," as well as an unusual choice: a cover version of "Flying," an obscure Lennon & McCartney instrumental from the Beatles' album *Magical Mystery Tour*. *DownBeat* called the record "languid but exhilarating," giving it four stars. The other four Embryo releases were not as successful, but generally received positive reviews as well.

But jazz critics' reactions to Herbie's new forays into jazz-rock were not universally positive. Bob Blumenthal, writing in *Philadelphia After Dark*, declared Herbie "one of the dullest and most uncreative 'stars' jazz has produced." He went on to say that Herbie was melodically limited while his flute playing was shrill, his tone unpleasant, and his ideas poorly executed. Blumenthal wasn't alone in his opinion of Herbie's abilities, but there was no denying the fact that whatever Herbie was doing, it was successful with the public; at the time Embryo was being planned, Herbie had five albums on *Billboard*'s best-selling jazz albums chart, was continuing his reign as the favorite flutist in *DownBeat*'s Readers Poll, and shared *Record World*'s Top Male Jazz Artist honors with Isaac Hayes.

In the fall, Embryo announced the impending release of seven more albums, with Herbie wandering even further afield from jazz than before. Among the albums being readied for release were works by Floating Opera, Anima, and Tonto's Expanding Head Band, all pop-rock groups. In response to the usual questions from jazz critics, Herbie responded while trying to restrain his impatience and anger, "As long as music is honest, why eliminate other kinds of valid expression? If I hear a trio of elephants, they'll let me record it."

By this time, he had grown tired of the musical antics of Sonny Sharrock and Steve Marcus, who were dismissed in September; Sharrock went off to work with Miles Davis, and Marcus moved into Woody Herman's jazz band. Longtime stalwarts Roy Ayers and Bruno Carr remained with Herbie. Of the dismissals, Herbie recounted the same restlessness he felt when being overwhelmed by his percussionists during his Afro-Cuban period:

> When Miroslav and Sonny joined the band, it was a great brand-new thing again, like finding a new food, you know? But as they developed their self-assurance, they started dominating the band, and once again, like when I had the African drummers, I felt like a sideman in my own group. The group wasn't expressing my personality anymore. The group I had had five very strong individuals. Their personalities were contrary to mine, and I like

quiet, peaceful things. They were more musically boisterous. We would play everybody's music, but toward the end I'd kind of cringe.

By this time, Herbie was also tiring of touring and had cut back his personal appearances to weekends. "I would like to get to the point of one tour in the United States during the summertime and one European and Japanese tour, and that's it. I want to devote the rest of the year to Embryo. I've worked one hundred fifty days this year and it's the most I've ever worked."

Roy Ayers was the next to leave, late in 1970. "I pushed him out of the band," Herbie recalled. "I told him that he should be a leader, after spending eight or nine years in my band." The second Embryo album, *Memphis Two Step*, originally scheduled to be called *Back Home*, followed, recorded in September and November 1970. Originally, it was designed to be an all-acoustic album consisting of three guitars and two basses, but Herbie changed his mind and used a larger group, including a chorus of Memphis brass, a returning Roy Ayers (who played on the title track) and old friends Sonny Sharrock, Miroslav Vitouš, and Patato Valdes, who played on four other sides.

His next album, *Muscle Shoals Nitty Gritty*, completed the thought started with *Memphis Underground*. He recorded at the famed Muscle Shoals Sound Studios in Muscle Shoals, Alabama, using a local rhythm section to augment his group. It would be the last session for bassist Miroslav Vitouš, who soon after joined Joe Zawinul and Wayne Shorter in a new fusion band called Weather Report. (Both Vitouš and Sonny Sharrock returned to record briefly with Herbie in late 1970 and 1971.)

From late 1970 into the summer of 1971, Herbie toured with Air (originally spelled "Ayr"), a jazz-rock fusion band he was recording on Embryo that was led by keyboardist Tom Coppola and featured the blues-oriented vocals of Coppola's wife, Googie. Herbie recorded several tracks with Air on a forthcoming LP to be titled "Herbie Mann '71," but the album was never released.

By this time Herbie had replaced Sharrock with another guitarist who had more tangible ties to the rock world: Duane Allman. One of the most admired guitarists in rock, Allman was a founding member of the Allman Brothers Band, a celebrated and respected artist noted for his melodic playing on electric bottleneck guitar and passion for the blues. In June and July 1971, Allman participated in the session that resulted in Herbie's final Embryo album, *Push Push*, cut in New York City. Herbie recalled:

> *Push Push* was another attempt to continue that *Memphis Underground* identity. Originally, I wanted to use Duck Dunn and Al Jackson from Booker T. & the MGs. I had already contacted and gotten Duane Allman to be on the record, because he was a great blues guitar player. I had sat in with Delaney and Bonnie Bramlett in Central Park, and he was there, and I asked him if he'd like to play on my record, and he said sure.
>
> On the first day of the session, nothing was working. What it boiled down to was that, for some reason, Al Jackson felt uncomfortable. He didn't know what to play. I didn't know that he needed to have that kind of structure. Listening to Booker T. & the MGs, you'd think that he just went in and grooved. So he asked me what to play and I said, "When I ask somebody to play with me, I know what they've done and just let them play." And he said, "Well, I can't do that. I need to know what you want me to do." So I went into the booth with Arif Mardin and said, "What do we do?" He said, "I don't know." So I went to the bass player, Jerry Jemmott, and he told me that Aretha Franklin's band was coming back that night and in her band was Bernard Purdie and Chuck Rainey. I went back to Al and said, "Tomorrow we're doing some reggae tunes. Do you know how to do that?" He said, "No, I've never played reggae." So I said, "Here's what I'm going to do. I'm going to pay you off for the rest of the album." And Duck Dunn was doing a fine job, but I said, "I'm sorry, Duck, but I need to have two guys who play together." So Rainey and Purdie were brought in and we finished the album.

Push Push became one of the most successful albums of Herbie Mann's career. But a controversy surrounding the album's artwork called even more attention to the record than it normally would have. The cover showed a bare-chested Herbie, holding his flute, which rested seductively on his right shoulder. The illustration inside the album was even more inflammatory. When the gatefold album was opened up, it revealed an image of a naked couple in the missionary position. Herbie chuckled when asked about the provocative album design.

> It was the first jazz record that had a jazz musician showing skin on the cover. And Nesuhi Ertegun said to me, "Why are you killing this record with this cover?" I just said, "Trust me. This is what's going to happen in the industry." Remember this was before the Ohio Players' covers. Well, the cover of *Push Push* caused a scandal. Radio stations said, "Unless you change your ways, we're never going to play your music again." They thought it was pornography. Inside was a picture of a couple coupling, but you couldn't see anything. And then we printed it on flocking material so you could feel it. So it became a scandal. Well, it was a calculated scandal. The bottom line was that if the record wasn't happening, it didn't matter what was on the cover. The band was great. Richard Tee, Duane Allman, Cornell Dupree. We did "What's Going On" and "Hatikvah." Originally I was going to call the album *Push*, but Roberta Flack said, "You need another push." [*Laughs*]

On October 29, less than four months after recording *Push Push*, Duane Allman was killed after he swerved his motorcycle on a Macon, Georgia, highway to avoid hitting a car turning in front of him. Allman was just twenty-four years old.

By the end of 1971, Herbie ended his Embryo experiment. "It involved being in an office at Atlantic on a day-to-day basis," he told *DownBeat* in 1980. "I was signing up acts, becoming a businessman, and getting to the point where I wound up selling less than some of the others, such as a really good Brazilian album, which they had neither felt nor understood."

After Herbie left, Atlantic used the Embryo imprint for two more releases in 1977, one of which was produced by Herbie, an album titled *Up*, by British jazz/funk/fusion artists Jim Mullen and Dick Morrissey. The album was designed to capitalize on Herbie's *Discothèque* sound, with Morrissey assuming Herbie's role on flute. In producing the album, Herbie used members of the Average White Band for its rhythm section. (The AWB had recently had a huge dance hit, "Pick Up the Pieces.")

While he was running Embryo, Herbie produced many important

albums that helped document the nascent jazz-rock era, but none was commercially successful. In December 1971, he cleaned out his Embryo offices for good and went back to work for Atlantic. It wouldn't be the only time Herbie tried running his own label. The next time would be twenty years later.

22

BREAKUP

The dissolving of Embryo in 1971 was not the only breakup in Herbie's life. After fifteen tumultuous years of marriage to his wife, Ruth, he finally got a divorce. Daughter Claudia said:

> I remember one night he was on his way to the club where he had his stuff ready before he would go out on tour. And I said, "What are you going to bring back for me, Daddy?" And he leaned down and said to us, "I'm not going to be living here anymore. I still love you and it's not your fault."

By that time, Herbie was already having an affair with an attractive, intelligent woman named Jan Cloonts, whom he had met while on one of his tours. Claudia Mann recalled:

> Jan was a flight attendant. He took one look at her and fell in love. He always liked women with short, red hair. That described my mother and it also described Janeal. Red hair.
>
> Jan and my father were together before my mother let him get divorced. My mother was a tough cookie. She had stipulations he needed to satisfy in order for her to release him to Jan. My mother was smart. She made him take out a huge insurance policy so that if anything happened to him, she would get everything and not Jan.

On June 5, 1970, Herbie and Jan had a daughter they named Laura. The divorce was extremely stressful on Herbie, who was also feeling tremendous guilt because of what the constant battles between him and Ruth were doing to their children, Paul and Claudia. He confided in Pat Rebillot about his troubles, who later said:

Herbie was never one to look back in any kind of anguish about anything except his first marriage. I never knew him to regret anything. He was always very positive about most things and that carried him a long way.

But Herbie's third wife, Janeal, had plenty to say about Ruth Mann:

Herbie's first wife Ruth was a hideous, repugnant human being. I'm sorry, but she was a bitch. A really nasty human being. When they went on their honeymoon, Herbie told me that she wanted to go out with some other guy. Herbie cried and begged her not to do it.

She was also a major alcoholic. He would come home and find her drunk all the time. The kids would be in bed and she'd be screaming and yelling at him at four o'clock in the morning, berating him, belittling him. That was an interesting side of Herbie, when you think about it. This was the first woman he chose. When she died, I said, "Ding, dong, the witch is dead." I really did, and did not feel badly at all about it, because I think she really ruined Paul and Claudia's life. She would call and haunt Herbie for years about the money and the alimony. She was just a real piece of work.

Jan was a stewardess and a very nice person, but I don't think Jan ever got Herbie at all. They were people that had two completely different approaches to life. She was monochrome and he was very colorful. Jan was pregnant before they got married. Laura, their first child, was actually at their wedding.

Late in 1970, Herbie and Ruth's divorce was finalized, and Herbie and Jan got married on July 11, 1971. On January 10, 1974, Jan gave birth to their second child, Herbie's fourth, whom they named Geoffrey. With

Herbie with *conguero* Ray Mantilla, c. 1960. Courtesy of MCG Jazz.

Herbie displayed part of his collection of ethnic flutes on the cover of his 1961 Atlantic album, *The Family of Mann*. From the author's collection.

Herbie receiving his fourth of thirteen straight awards as favorite flutist of readers of *DownBeat* magazine. Making the presentation is actor Laurence Harvey; Herbie scored Harvey's narration of Walter Benton's *This Is My Beloved*, 1961. Photo by PoPsie Randolph. Used by permission. Courtesy of Janeal Arison.

Arriving in Rio de Janeiro, July 1961. Courtesy of Janeal Arison.

Historic record date in Rio de Janeiro, October 17, 1962: Herbie Mann with Antônio Carlos Jobim at the piano and Baden Powell on guitar. It was at this session Jobim first recorded "One Note Samba." Courtesy of MCG Jazz.

Herbie Mann at the Village Gate, the 1961 live concert, and Herbie's breakthrough to the mainstream, which featured his hit, "Comin' Home Baby." From the author's collection.

Herbie with longtime *conguero* Carlos "Patato" Valdes, early 1960s. Courtesy of Janeal Arison.

The cover of this 1963 songbook shows Herbie in what Willis Conover described as a "half-hula" stance. From the author's collection.

Playing a handmade flute in Japan in the 1960s. Courtesy of Janeal Arison.

雅楽とモダンジャズ

GAGAKU Meets Jazz-Flutist HERBIE-MANN

迎賓館

Ad for a September 1964 concert at the Shirogane Geihin-Kan, outside of Tokyo, which combined Herbie Mann's group with traditional *gagaku* music and dance. Courtesy of Janeal Arison.

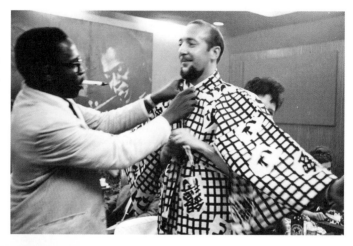

"He was always a fashion plate," Herbie's sister Judi said. A content Herbie gets fitted with traditional Japanese garb, prior to a performance in Japan, 1960s. Courtesy of Janeal Arison.

Marvin Israel's psychedelic art design graces the cover of *The Wailing Dervishes* (1967), recorded at the Village Theater in New York. From the author's collection.

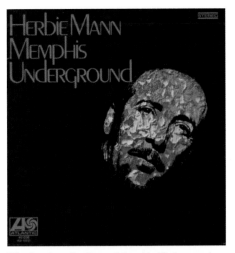

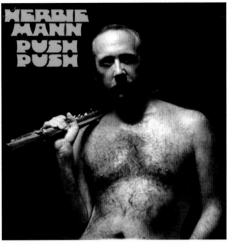

The landmark album *Memphis Underground* (1969), in which Herbie Mann turned his attention to R&B and soul. From the author's collection.

This controversial cover for the album *Push Push* (1971) "caused a scandal," Herbie said, "but it was a calculated scandal." From the author's collection.

Herbie being interviewed by Japanese reporters, 1974. To his right is his second wife, Jan. Courtesy of Janeal Arison.

In England, early 1970s. Flair Photography Ltd. Courtesy of Janeal Arison.

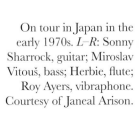

On tour in Japan in the early 1970s. *L–R*: Sonny Sharrock, guitar; Miroslav Vitouš, bass; Herbie, flute; Roy Ayers, vibraphone. Courtesy of Janeal Arison.

The Family of Mann, 1974. Clockwise from left: Tony Levin, Sam Brown, Pat Rebillot, Herbie Mann, David Newman, Steve Gadd, Armen Halburian. Photo by Joel Brodsky.

"Hi-Jack" 45 rpm single. From the author's collection.

Jasil Brazz album cover, 1987. From the author's collection.

With Ivan Lins, Herbie's favorite modern Brazilian composer, c. 1990s. Courtesy of Janeal Arison.

Liner photo for the *Peace Pieces* CD, 1995. Photo by Valerie Santagto.

Herbie the hockey fan, playing "The Star-Spangled Banner" at a Pittsburgh Penguins game in 1992. Photo by Bob Bowman. Courtesy of MCG Jazz.

Herbie's first wife, Ruth, and their children, Paul and Claudia, c. 1980. Courtesy of Judi Solomon Kennedy.

With daughter Laura, 1990s. Courtesy of Judi Solomon Kennedy.

Herbie (right) at his mother's ninetieth birthday celebration, 1995. *L–R*: Niece Debra Kennedy Compton, son Geoff Mann, daughter Laura Mann Lepik, and third wife Janeal Arison. Courtesy of Judi Solomon Kennedy.

Janeal and Herbie on their wedding day on September 8, 1991. Courtesy of Janeal Arison.

With his sister Judi, Sandestin, Florida, October 1998. Courtesy of Judi Solomon Kennedy.

With the author, showing off construction of his new guest house, Santa Fe, New Mexico, December 1, 1999. From the author's collection.

Herbie's final concert at the New Orleans Jazz & Heritage Festival, May 3, 2003. *L–R*: Ricky Sebastian, Larry Coryell, Chuck Rainey, Herbie, David Newman, Mark Soskin. Courtesy of Janeal Arison.

With Phil Woods at the *Beyond Brooklyn* session, November 2002. Courtesy of MCG Jazz.

After making his last recording, "Time After Time," with Marty (*left*) and Jay Ashby (*right*), Phoenix, Arizona, May 2003. Courtesy of MCG Jazz.

Herbie acknowledges the crowd after his final public performance at the New Orleans Jazz & Heritage Festival, May 3, 2003. Courtesy of Judi Solomon Kennedy.

With Janeal after recording "Time After Time." Courtesy of MCG Jazz.

their father away, Paul and Claudia were brought up by Jan, who nurtured them in ways they never got from Ruth. Claudia recalled:

Jan was the opposite of my father. She was super, super, super mellow. It took a lot to rattle her. She was a great stepmother and the best mom, and gave me the discipline I needed. She really shaped me.

But it was crazy how the women would throw themselves at my dad. It didn't matter if I was with him or not, and I was his daughter. This is a really funny story. One time he was renting a place in Acapulco and Merv Griffin was living in a house directly above him on a hill, off to one side. Merv liked being outside and they used to wave to each other all the time. Soon after my dad got there, Merv saw my dad go outside and help a woman get into a taxi. After it left, he just stood there in the driveway. Just then, another taxi came up, and another woman got out, and they went into the house together. Within twenty-four hours of arriving, my father had three women coming and going from his house. When the third one left, Merv, who was gay, was standing out on his balcony again and just started applauding.

He was also the coolest dad in the world because we got to go to Atlantic Records and get as many albums as we wanted. Jan made him stop doing drugs. He wasn't an addict or anything, but he could take a couple of puffs on a joint or blow a line of cocaine and then not do it again for a long time.

My father was a real clotheshorse and he was very vain, so when contact lenses came out, he got those. He always looked real good and was very charismatic. It was the sixties and seventies, and he used to wear those pencil-thin pants. He looked like a total hipster. But he was a good guy and was always thoughtful about other people.

With his personal life finally settling down, Herbie moved on into the 1970s, still riding high on the successes of *Memphis Underground* and *Push Push*. His run, however, as *DownBeat's* favorite flutist in its annual Readers Poll ended after thirteen consecutive years, as his records were getting further afield from mainstream jazz. By now, it didn't matter, for Herbie had achieved his goal of crossing over to the mainstream. He was now attracting larger audiences than he ever had, and his popularity extended around the world. After fifteen years of tumult and anxiety in his battles with Ruth, his new marriage with Jan stabilized his family life for the time being. In the early seventies, his professional life settled down as well, as he formed a new band that would serve him well for the rest of the decade.

23

MANN OF THE WORLD

The Embryo experiment lasted almost two years, an interval that was getting to be a regular signal for change in Herbie's career. Both his experiments in Afro-Cuban and Brazilian had lasted that long before he became restless and proceeded to the next idea on the horizon. "Every time a style of music I'm playing gets a little too perfect," he told interviewer Norman Schreiber, "and by perfect, I mean something that is a little too tidy, something that is in a box instead of on a meadow. With me, this happens about every two years or so. When it happens, I change."

In 1972, Herbie left the development of jazz-rock fusion to Miles Davis and returned to playing more mainstream jazz, but still with a decidedly R&B flavor. Part of the stabilizing of his band, now being called the Family of Mann, was due to the presence of two key musicians who would play in his group for years: Pat Rebillot on keyboards and David "Fathead" Newman on tenor saxophone. Newman, who also played flute, proved to be a great musical foil for Herbie, and they would often play "dueling flutes" together onstage. Newman was heavily influenced by soul music, always a favorite of Herbie's, so he kept that element in the band that Herbie had been wanting since he first heard Ray Charles's music in the late 1950s. Newman joined in time to play with Herbie at the Montreux Jazz Festival in June and then the New York Jazz Festival at Yankee Stadium in July. Songs from both of these appeared on the album *Hold On, I'm Comin'*.

The bearded, balding Rebillot was the first keyboardist Herbie ever employed regularly in his band, and also served as his arranger, conductor, and "straw boss." He played for Herbie for the next five years. Rebillot recalled:

> I used to do a lot of studio work at Atlantic Records, and I was doing something with Carly Simon and Herbie heard me, and after the session said, "What do you do when you're not working with her?" I wasn't her sideman, I was just playing her record date. So I said, "Just more record dates." And he asked me to join his band. I was just finishing a stint with Gary Burton and I thought Herbie would be more fun than Gary, so I switched over. Herbie let me surround myself with five or six different kinds of keyboards, so that was what was fun for me. I played clavinet, electric piano, acoustic piano, a Hammond B-3 organ, a Mellotron, and a small synth.
>
> When I joined him, Bruno Carr was playing drums, but he was ready to make a change. So Herbie asked me for recommendations, and from then on, I would recommend people to him. I knew the best studio musicians available who could play jazz.

By this time, Herbie had long since abandoned playing clubs, preferring less frequent appearances at festivals and stadiums. He said later:

> I let the albums do the traveling for me because I didn't like to go on the road. I felt like it wasn't necessary to be on the road fifty weeks a year. If you make a record, the record does the traveling, and then if it's successful, you can get compensated and play concerts rather than play clubs. The perfect mix would be to have a hit record, go on the road to sell the record, and then more people see you and buy more records, and when they buy more records, you get better money. But if you value quality of life more than this endless cycle, you make decisions on what you want your career to be.

Herbie's latest musical excursion was reggae, which he started experimenting with as early as December 1971, when he recorded "Never Ending Song of Love," which ended up on the 1973 *Turtle Bay* album (named for a garden district in midtown Manhattan where the United Nations building stands).

It had been two years since Embryo folded, and Herbie was getting characteristically restless again. He was getting frustrated with Atlantic, especially in the wake of the failure of Embryo and, for the first time, was actually thinking about leaving the label. He recalled:

> Nesuhi Ertegun was my conduit there. He was my producer and my confidant. Now I was feeling very, very aggressive about money and a contract, and I was ready to leave Atlantic and go with Arista. I went up to Atlantic one day just to see some of my friends and Davey Glew, who later became the head of Epic. He was with Atlantic at the time, and saw me and said, "Have you signed yet?" I said, "No, but I think I'm going to sign with Arista on Monday." So he went in to see Ahmet Ertegun and Ahmet called me up, had breakfast with me at his house. After breakfast, he said, "What do you need to get for you to stay?" So I told him and I stayed. Then he said, "Nesuhi has given up, so now I'm your guy. What do you want to do?" I said, "Let's go to London and do an English version of *Memphis Underground* using rock musicians."

So in 1973, Herbie and Pat Rebillot went to England and recorded for a week at London's Advision Studios. Ahmet Ertegun was able to get British rock guitarists Mick Taylor and Albert Lee to sit in on the session. Taylor, a former member of John Mayall's Bluesbreakers, was then a member of the Rolling Stones, while Lee was already a much-in-demand session musician, as well as being a member of the British rock band Heads Hands & Feet. The session, which resulted in the Atlantic album *London Underground*, featured cover versions of such British rock staples as the Stones' "Bitch," Traffic's "Paper Sun," the Beatles' "You Never Give Me Your Money," Derek and the Dominos' "Layla," and Procol Harum's "A Whiter Shade of Pale." Pat Rebillot recalled:

> He would have fantasies about playing with the Rolling Stones. Herbie didn't have any difficulties thinking of himself as a star. He liked to travel first-class while the rest of us were in coach. We would

gather at his apartment and he would rent a limo to take us to the airport. He lived on Fifth Avenue and 79th Street, and after that, moved a little north of the Metropolitan Museum of Art.

London Underground was highlighted by a cameo appearance by legendary Django Reinhardt compatriot Stéphane Grappelli, who played violin on a jaunty version of Donovan's "Mellow Yellow," on which Albert Lee assumed Reinhardt's role. Herbie recalled:

> I had thought all along that Donovan's "Mellow Yellow" sounded like a Hot Club of France tune, and lo and behold, Stéphane was playing at Ronnie Scott's that week. So we got him. Then we were going to do a reggae tune for the album and we heard that the Jimmy Cliff band was in town. So we ended up doing a whole album with the Jimmy Cliff band.

Pat Rebillot recalled:

> Herbie treated Stéphane with reverence; he was so awed by him. At one point, there was some kind of miscommunication that resulted in Grappelli not getting something right, and I was getting a little frustrated, but Herbie said, "Shhh. Never mind. He's Stéphane Grappelli."

The Cliff band was led by Jamaican saxophonist Tommy McCook, a veteran reggae and ska musician. Mick Taylor and Albert Lee stuck around for that session also, which produced enough material for two albums—but only one, titled *Reggae*, was issued in the United States. The cover illustration, by Don Brautigam, showed Herbie hoisting an armful of flutes, and in the background a horse-drawn carriage carrying the figure of Ahmet Ertegun in the backseat, with the Atlantic logo on the carriage's back.

The highlight of the *Reggae* album was an eighteen-minute jam on Smokey Robinson's Motown classic "My Girl," on which both Taylor and Lee were let loose for extended solos behind a contagious groove by the McCook band.

A second album, *Reggae II*, was released in New Zealand and later in Japan, but never in the U.S. The first reggae album had done well enough to warrant a sequel, and Herbie and Rebillot traveled to Kingston, Jamaica, later that year to join the McCook band to record four more tracks. The session was fortified by the pungent scent of native marijuana, smoked by two of the Jamaican musicians hired for the session, keyboardists Gladstone Anderson and Winston Wright. The cover art for this album was repeated for Herbie's 1981 Atlantic album, *Mellow*. Pat Rebillot recalled:

> He wanted a Motown sound. He liked playing "Never Can Say Goodbye" and songs like that. I had been working with Bob Babbitt and Andrew Smith, so they joined us for a while before we went to London. But Herbie got tired of that rather quickly and wanted to stretch out again. So I tried to get him some stylists who could cover more ground.

Upon returning home, Herbie started building his new Family of Mann. With Rebillot's help, Herbie selected a stalwart group of solid studio musicians that served as the nucleus of Herbie's musical activities for the rest of the 1970s. The initial members of the Family included Sam Brown on guitar, David Newman on tenor sax and flute, Tony Levin on bass, Armen Halburian on percussion, and Steve Gadd on drums. (Brown was soon replaced by Jerry Friedman.) Rebillot recalled, "I hipped him to Steve Gadd and Tony Levin, and when he heard them play, he said, 'Wow, where have you been keeping these guys?'"

On their first album as a unit, titled *First Light*, Herbie shared the spotlight with the band, with all but Halburian contributing compositions. In deference to the unity of the band, Herbie's name doesn't appear on the album cover, only the group's name. "He was very generous in giving us space and letting us do our thing," Rebillot said. "I quickly became his 'straw boss' because Herbie wasn't skilled at writing music down, so he really needed somebody like me who had the technical chops to do that and make arrangements for him. He didn't pay us well, but he paid us enough, and we were happy with that."

On *First Light*, Herbie took a backseat to the other musicians, something he had never done before, and the result was one of the most satisfying and varied albums of his career. Highlights included Brown's funky "Sunrise Highs"; Gadd's lovely tribute to his newborn daughter, "Lullaby for Mary Elizabeth," which he played on an African thumb piano known as a *kalimba*; and Herbie's own delightful, Latin-flavored composition "Mexicali."

The Family of Mann was more than a family in name only. The band members got to know each other well and became closer than any musicians Herbie had hired previously, especially Newman and Rebillot. When Rebillot got married for the first time, on New Year's Day 1974, Herbie sent him a bromeliad plant with a note attached that said, "I hope you know what you're doing." Rebillot recalled:

> The thing that really haunted him was his divorce from Ruth. He had a miserable time with her and talked about it incessantly because it was driving him crazy. I'm not sure of the details, but this nasty, nasty divorce lasted for years and years. That put a crimp in things while I was with him. It was a horrible denouement that just took forever to get over.

Herbie tried getting Rebillot interested in professional ice hockey. A rabid fan of the New York Rangers, he talked Rebillot into going to a game between the Rangers and the Boston Bruins. "I wasn't a hockey guy," Rebillot said. "Football and baseball were my sports."

For two weeks in April 1974, the Family of Mann toured Japan. Japanese music was Herbie's latest passion, and he was especially excited at the prospect of playing with Japanese musicians. He told *DownBeat:*

> I had been wanting to do something with Japanese music for a long time, but on all five of my trips there, I was so involved in business that I couldn't really get into it. This year I immersed myself in the Japanese culture as much as I possibly could. Our concerts were over at 8:30 every night so we would go eat some kind of raw fish and other Japanese delicacies and I'd go home and write for four hours. I was reading Japanese poetry and literature and listening to their music constantly and absorbing their art.

While in Japan, Herbie and his band recorded an album of Japanese art music with Minoru Muraoka and His New Dimension, a popular Japanese group that played modern music on traditional Japanese instruments. The album *Gagaku & Beyond* featured three traditional Japanese tunes, plus one original composition by Herbie (the title track, Herbie's attempt at writing a Japanese melody, which he recorded with just his band), and one by Rebillot, the atmospheric and beautiful "Mauve Over Blues," one of the more enchanting selections Herbie ever recorded.

Gagaku was one of two forms of Japanese instrumental art music dating back to the eighth century. The other was *shomyo*, a traditional Buddhist chant, an example of which was performed on the album by the Modern Shomyo Study Group, four monks who often sang with Muraoka and who belonged to the Nishihongan-ji set of Shingon-Shu. Herbie's flute blended perfectly with the monks as well as with Muraoka's end-blown notched bamboo flute, called the *shakuhachi*.

Gagaku & Beyond was recorded in Tokyo for the Finnadar label, distributed in the United States by Atlantic, and released in 1976. It was probably the most esoteric album Herbie recorded in his career, laden with the moody chanting of the monks and strange sounds coming from the traditional instruments played by the Ono Gagaku Society. It was his ultimate experiment in fusion.

Three songs were left over from the session. "Anata" was a multimillion-selling hit in Japan, so Herbie overdubbed a vocal by sixteen-year-old Akiko Kosaka. Two of the songs were supposed to be part of a five-song Japanese equivalent of "African Suite," described by Herbie as "an anthology of the evolution of Japanese music." The Japanese session was initially supposed to produce a double album titled *The Butterfly in a Stone Garden* after one of the songs. Instead, only one album was issued, with the remaining three songs released on Herbie's 1976 Atlantic album *Surprises*.

During the concerts in Japan, Pat Rebillot remembered the band getting a kick out of how Herbie was introduced: "Herbie Mann: America's Number One Fruit." Herbie socialized with the Family of Mann more than with his previous groups, who would often scatter after recording sessions or concerts. Rebillot recalled:

We were known as "The Band That Likes to Eat." We had a

lot of meals together. One that I particularly remember, which is a good example of our habits, was when we were in Tokyo. There must have been around ten of us, the members of the band and a couple of the wives. We went down to eat in this nice hotel dining room, and about halfway through dinner, we realized that the whole staff was standing around, staring at us. Finally, we asked what was going on and somebody explained that they couldn't believe that all of these Americans were using chopsticks and doing it right.

Herbie and I were the ringleaders when it came to food. He would often pay me in dinners when I would help him work out a new song and harmonize his melodies. I worked on the cheap that way, but I didn't mind. He was quite the epicurean and I was right there with him, always willing to try new things.

Herbie was pathbreaking with what he did with the flute. He wasn't to every critic's taste, but he hewed his own path. What astonishes me today is that so much music consists of one chord. He anticipated that all those years ago. It used to drive me crazy, playing one chord, but he was ahead of the curve with that.

He had a very strong self-image and liked to flaunt it. He liked the women to like him, and a lot of them did go for his kind of image. I remember one of his favorite lines at his concerts was that at the end of the show, wherever we were, he'd say that he wanted to move there.

Upon returning to the U.S., the Family of Mann attended a record date in June to record other Japanese-oriented songs, but none was ever released. He toyed with the idea of making a record in Nashville with country musicians, but it never came off. By the end of the year, Herbie was ready to turn the page again, this time making one of the most controversial musical decisions of his career.

Herbie Mann was going disco.

24

HIJACKED

At the end of 1974, Herbie, who always had his ear to the ground for new trends, decided that the propulsive dance music that was becoming known as disco would be the next big wave of the 1970s. To test the market, he recorded a single with the Family of Mann. The song on the A-side was "Hi-Jack," written by a Spanish drummer/songwriter named Fernando Arbex for his band Barrabás. The B-side side was "The Orient Express," a funk-rock tune written by Pat Rebillot that had an offbeat melody and catchy dance rhythm, which went unheard on radio, as most promotional 45s sent to disc jockeys during the seventies had the A-side on both sides of the record. (Characteristically, two versions of "Hi-Jack" appeared on promotional 45s: the uncut version on one side, which ran five minutes and thirty-two seconds, and an edited version on the other, which ran three minutes.) "The Orient Express" never appeared on an album and is one of the hidden gems of Herbie's discography. "Hi-Jack," on the other hand, became the biggest hit of Herbie Mann's career. Pat Rebillot recalled:

Herbie wanted to jump on the disco bandwagon, so he gave me a version of a song. But it turned out to be the wrong side of the record, so I had to do the one he wanted as well, which turned out to be "Hi-Jack." We managed to pull it together very quickly, and it became a hit for him. I think certain aspects of disco appealed to him, like the simplicity of it and its steady beat.

When "Hi-Jack" came out, it became an instantaneous hit, surprising everyone, but the most surprised of all was Herbie. The record went to No. 1 on *Billboard*'s disco charts and No. 14 on its pop charts, becoming a million seller. Suddenly, Herbie became an attraction for an entirely new generation of fans, few of whom had grown up with jazz or Herbie's music in their lives.

The popularity of "Hi-Jack" resulted in Atlantic having Herbie record a full album of dance-oriented songs titled *Discothèque*. Longer dance mixes, then just coming into style, were also made of the song. For the first time, Herbie used a vocal group on his records: a female trio consisting of Cissy Houston, Sylvia Shemwell, and Eunice Peterson. Herbie had cannily added the trio because its unison vocal sound was prominent in many disco hits he was hearing on the radio, most notably "T.S.O.P. (The Sound of Philadelphia)," by the Three Degrees with the studio band MFSB.

Herbie's daughter Claudia remembered:

> With "Hi-Jack," he finally got the attention he wanted for all those years, but not for playing jazz. He got it for disco. He thought everyone was going to be happy for him to have this big hit, but no, everyone totally turned on him and it made him very upset. Years later, when Jennifer Lopez came out with "Jenny from the Block," he said, "I'm going to sue her." I laughed and said, "You can't sue J-Lo, Dad!"

"Jenny from the Block" was released in September 2002, less than a year before Herbie died. The song featured a sample of a melody Herbie played on "Hi-Jack," but the sample came from a recording by Enoch Light and the Light Brigade and not from Herbie's Atlantic recording. After looking into the possibilities of an infringement lawsuit, and realizing a legal battle at this stage would further jeopardize his already failing health, he decided to drop it altogether. Even though Lopez was making millions off his playing, Herbie had no rights to either the song or the performance, and as a good businessman, knew he wouldn't have much of a case. (In addition to "Hi-Jack," other recordings by Herbie were sampled over the years. "Bijou," from *Latin Mann*, was sampled by hip-hop group the Pharcyde for their song "Pack the Pipe." British singer-songwriter Dido used "Cajun Moon" from the 1973 *Surprises* album for her song "Thank You." Other songs that were sampled included "Push Push," "Summertime," from *Herbie Mann at the Village Gate*, "Today," and, of course, "Memphis Underground," the latter used by three prominent hip-hop acts: Ice Cube, 3rd Bass, and Salt-n-Pepa.)

The souring of Herbie's relationship with Atlantic began after "Hi-Jack" became a hit. Herbie attributes this to structural changes going on at the company, which saw in "Hi-Jack" the golden egg the goose laid and wanted more. Herbie recalled:

> Between *Push Push* and leaving, I made a disco hit called "Hi-Jack." It was a choice I made. I really didn't want to do a fusion record because I really didn't feel comfortable, and I figured that if I was going to do a formula record, I might as well do one that might sell. So I made a top ten record. After that, whatever critics were left who thought that maybe there was some chance, they gave up on me. That was it.
>
> I had a record that was played every fifteen minutes on the radio. There was a new regime at Atlantic and that's what they wanted me to do. So I did a bunch of disco records. Then fusion started coming in, but I didn't want to play that way. That concept of groove was not the concept of groove I grew up with. I wanted steady. I wanted R&B. I wanted Latin. I wanted intensity. I wanted heat. And I didn't think that music did that.

A trio of albums followed the release of *Discothèque*, but only one could be viewed as disco. *Waterbed* (1975) was the first, an intoxicating blend of R&B and funk that became a popular record in black dance clubs. In *DownBeat*'s review, Pete Welding praised the album for what it was—"attractive, uncomplicated, funky, and unabashedly commercial dance"—but also said there was virtually no jazz content, originality, or imagination in the record.

In 1976, Atlantic issued *Surprises*, which included a blend of styles Herbie had been courting in recent years, but again, no disco. *Surprises* made Cissy Houston more prominent; she was given billing on the cover of the album just below Herbie's name. Two of Houston's vocals, J. J. Cale's sultry "Cajun Moon" and the Brazilian standard "Asa Branca," featured sensuous, evocative arrangements by Pat Rebillot. The album also included the three songs from the aborted Japanese suite recorded in 1973.

Only *Bird in a Silver Cage*, issued in 1976, could be considered a disco follow-up to *Discothèque*. Herbie recorded it in Munich, Germany, using a string ensemble from the Munich Philharmonic Orchestra and filling out the sound with an insistent dance beat and background voices to emulate the dance craze currently sweeping Germany.

Cissy Houston, probably the best thing Herbie had going for him during this time, departed for a solo career at the end of 1976. As Pat Rebillot recalled: "I remember Cissy's last night with us in Kansas City in this great arena in the round. It was as if she was saving it all for that night. It was astonishing how well she sang; it was one of the best nights with a singer I've ever had."

But the rut Herbie was stuck in continued, as Atlantic continued to try and mine the detritus of "Hi-Jack." In 1977 and 1978, pressure from the suits at Atlantic resulted in three additional disco albums: *Fire Island*, *Super Mann*, and *Yellow Fever*, the last featuring an embarrassing attempt at turning "Comin' Home Baby" into a disco dance hit. Each of the three albums featured the same pounding disco beat and female background chorus. The Family of Mann made its last appearance in 1978 on *Brazil— Once Again*, Herbie's attempt to revive his Brazilian sound. One of the highlights of the album was a tribute to Brazilian soccer star Pelé. Herbie said that the song reflected "my concept of the way Pelé flows down a soccer field. We overdubbed stadium sounds to give it the feel of a soccer match." The album was at least listenable to his fans who hadn't already been turned off by his disco albums, but it was merely Atlantic's final token gesture to appease Herbie.

But Herbie was still adamant about going his own way, and he and the moguls at Atlantic continued to butt heads over the direction his musical career was taking. With *Brazil—Once Again*, Herbie rediscovered his love for Brazilian music. In 1978, he told the *New York Daily News*:

> When Brazilian music first came on, it was a beautiful, sophisticated white version of samba, but it was strictly a white commodity. What you're getting now is a blacker Brazilian music.

It's funkier, has more soul to it, and it's much more exciting. I mean, I love bossa nova, but I think that it was just an aperitif and that this is gonna be the main course.

I happen to have enough guts to make records that are enjoyed by the mass of people. That's my taste. I don't give a damn about *DownBeat* or NARAS awards or anybody. I happen to like the music I play.

At the end of the year, Pat Rebillot departed also, and Herbie had to resort to using studio musicians and finding other arrangements himself. He said later:

They wanted me to do this record called *Super Mann*. And I said to them, "You know what? You want me to do this record? You pick the tunes. You pick the musicians. I'll do the solos and leave." It's the only time I ever gave up control. Even though the record sold well, it didn't sell that much better than the Brazilian record. So that was about the end.

Herbie made one more record for Atlantic, 1979's *Sunbelt*, before terminating his twenty-year association with Atlantic. He recalled wistfully:

Twenty years is a long time from being the fair-haired boy and being able to do what you want to. For many different reasons, it wasn't working anymore. So it was time to leave. I should have left five years earlier. I tried other labels, but nobody was interested. By switching over to being an instrumental pop artist, there was no longevity factor anymore. The MJQ probably didn't sell as many records as I did, but they kept their audience and they didn't change, so the audience went with them. I was always challenging my audience and asking them to change too.

I think the disco records did it. But also, the business was changing. Yuppies and West Coast fusion music were coming in. The Jazz Crusaders were getting played on California stations, even easy listening stations. And even though a lot of my music was easy listening jazz, it didn't fit into the "formula." I didn't want to be formularized. And I didn't want anybody telling me that this was the sound you need to do to get your record played on the air. Excuse me, I still think that I have to do what I think is right for me.

25

JANEAL

With no record deal, Herbie's next album was a vanity project, recorded on his own label, Herbie Mann Music, with Herbie selling copies himself at concert appearances. The album was recorded live in a direct-to-disc recording made during an appearance at the Great American Music Hall in San Francisco in September 1980. In keeping with his innovative instincts, Herbie used a Roland Chorus Echo Machine to create a variety of effects for his flute on the two extended cuts recorded that day: an astonishingly inventive rendition of Miles Davis's "All Blues" and a song he co-wrote with bassist Frank Gravis called "Forest Rain." In addition to Gravis, Herbie's band consisted solely of percussionist Armen Halburian, the lone carryover from the Family of Mann, and Bangladeshi tabla player Badal Roy.

Three more albums were issued by Atlantic in two-year intervals after Herbie's disassociation with the label, although all were one-offs, with Herbie earning a flat fee with no contract. The first, *Mellow*, issued in 1981, was a hodgepodge of recordings left over from the 1970s. Not only were the recordings recycled, so was the cover art; Atlantic used the same Don Brautigam illustration employed on the *Reggae II* album, which was never released in the United States.

Mellow included a remake of "Memphis Underground," recorded at the 1977 Montreux Jazz Festival, with old friends Larry Coryell, David Newman, Richard Tee, and the Brecker Brothers (Michael and Randy) in the band. Two other songs were unissued titles from Herbie's second reggae session in Jamaica in 1973. Bob Marley's "Bend Down Low" featured background vocals overdubbed around 1978 by Cissy Houston and her fifteen-year-old daughter Whitney. The song is noteworthy not just for the appearance of Whitney Houston, but also since it was sung by Herbie himself, the one-and-only vocal of his career. Whitney Houston was still a few years away from her own career breakthrough, but years later, when Herbie was reminded of this, he chuckled.

> She was singing background. You can't tell it's her. She was just the fifteen-year-old daughter of Cissy, who used to sing with me. One day after she became famous I went to a record store and the guy behind the counter said, "Can you reissue the album and have it say "featuring Whitney Houston"? I laughed. Of course! There will be no problem here. All you gotta do is call it *Where's Whitney?* like *Where's Waldo?* I said no.

Astral Island, issued in 1983, was noteworthy only for Herbie's last recorded credit as a tenor saxophonist, although he took no solos during any of the songs. His last ever recording for Atlantic, 1985's *See Through Spirits*, featured members of a new band, dominated by guitarist O'Donel Levy, who wrote half of the songs on the record and contributed vocals to two of them.

It was becoming evident that Herbie, now in his fifties, had passed his prime and was struggling to find a sound and an audience. By this time, jazz had become directionless; fusion had worn out its welcome, and Herbie had neither the temperament nor the incentive for exploration he used to have.

> After I left Atlantic, I didn't have a record contract and I was living on Park Avenue, pretending I was the most successful jazz musician in the world. The records I made on my own didn't do very well, and I was still trying to do the same kind of music. I had a band with Badal Roy, Naná Vasconcelos, and Frank Gravis. Then I had a band with Buddy Williams, and then a band with a Baltimore guitarist named O'Donel Levy. But I was struggling.

And then he met Janeal.

Born in 1952, Susan Janeal Arison was a commercial television actress who became a jazz fan when her father took her to see a performance by Ella Fitzgerald at the Carter Barron Amphitheatre in Washington, D.C. It was July 4, 1967. Also on the bill were guitarist Charlie Byrd and flutist Herbie Mann. Janeal was only fifteen at the time, but five years later, when she began attending college at the University of Maryland's campus in Munich, Germany, she remembered something special about Herbie's performance, and while shopping at the PX, bought a copy of *Push Push* for $2.99. She recalled:

> I married this guy who was my psychology professor, who was very cerebral, but only listened to Mahler. He was nineteen years older than me. Herbie was twenty-two years older than me.
>
> In 1977 I was living in West Virginia and went to hear Herbie perform at Blues Alley. My husband didn't come with me because he wasn't interested, so I went with a friend. I actually saw him twice. I saw him a second time because I had to take my friend to the bus station so we decided to see Herbie again. This time we sat closer to the stage and I noticed a little flirtation thing going on between Herbie and me.

After the show, Herbie approached Janeal and asked her if she'd like to go to an Argentinean restaurant with the band, and she agreed. "It was like there was nobody else in the room," she recalled. "He actually had another woman who he was traveling with, but it was just him and me. The energy between us was just so intense." Nothing happened after the dinner, but Janeal kept thinking about the charismatic flute player.

The next year, Janeal and her husband split up, and when Herbie came to play at a small theater in Hagerstown, Maryland, Janeal went to see him again. On an impulse, she sent a note backstage, reminding Herbie of their Argentinean dinner, signing it "Susan."

> I went by the name Susan when I was an actress. Well, he came out on stage and the first thing he said was, "I'd like to play for you a song called "Yes, I'd Love to See You Again, Susan Blues" After the show, I spent the night with him and that was the beginning of our relationship. For nine years, I was "the other woman."

Although Herbie had done a lot of skirt chasing while married to both Ruth and Jan, after he met Janeal, all of that ended. After the affair had lasted seven years, Janeal ended the relationship. Herbie was experiencing a lot of guilt and Jan had supposedly hired an investigator to find out whom he had been seeing on such a regular basis. They were apart for two years before getting back together again. Janeal recalled:

That June, Herbie went to the funeral of a guy in the finance department at Atlantic Records. After the funeral, he got the realization that life was short and that he deserved to be loved. He went home that night and told Jan and that was it. We started living together after that.

Herbie never "took care of me." During the seven years we were together, I had a very successful career as a commercial television actress. I was the "Commercial Queen" of New York City at that time. He had his dips in his career and he was going through one of these at that time. He was actually hocking things to pay his bills. It got to the point where Jan suggested he pursue another career. Can you imagine that? Herbie Mann doing something besides playing the flute? We moved to Santa Fe in 1989, but if I hadn't had my money, we wouldn't have been able to buy our house, because he didn't have anything. He and Jan lived beyond their means. They lived on Park Avenue, their kids went to the most exclusive private schools and summer camps, and they had a live-in housekeeper.

In 1990, Herbie and Jan's divorce became final, although Jan appealed the decision twice. Herbie and Janeal married on September 14, 1991. He was sixty-one and she was thirty-nine. Herbie went through a big change after meeting Janeal. She recalled:

I think his ego got the better of him before I came along. I look at pictures of Herbie before he met me, and I hardly recognize him. He had this arrogance and a kind of swagger about him that was, to me, unappealing. I think that our love grounded him in a way that he hadn't had before. After we moved to Santa Fe, Herbie realized how much he loved being out in nature, which was really interesting because here was this Brooklyn city boy who really didn't like cities anymore. There were other things that changed in his life, like he loved getting up early in the morning when he didn't have to play clubs anymore. After we met, there was this other side that came out of him that I think was more "the essential Herbie."

He was born Jewish, but he wasn't religious at all. He pretty much scorned Judaism and all organized religion, but he was a very spiritual person, which went along well with me because I am an unapologetic atheist.

Janeal described Herbie as "one of the world's greatest hedonists." The two of them shared their love for nature, fine dining, and enjoyed traveling to exotic places. As corny as it might sound, after two incompatible marriages, Herbie had finally found his soul mate and it changed him for the better. It may have been just a coincidence, but just as Herbie formed the Family of Mann after marrying Jan, he found another stable group of musicians at the same time he met Janeal. It happened as the result of a chance encounter at one of his favorite New York nightspots.

26

KOKOPELLI

In 1986, Herbie was performing at the Blue Note in New York, one of his regular haunts of the eighties and nineties. He had not made a record since *See Through Spirits* and was still without a recording contract. Also appearing at the Blue Note was the New York Samba Band, a quartet that included Brazilian guitarist Romero Lubambo. Born in Rio de Janeiro in 1955, Lubambo was a classically trained musician who learned piano before turning to classical guitar at the age of thirteen.

In 1985, Lubambo moved to the United States and formed a group that played modern Brazilian jazz. Lubambo recalled that during the week they played on the same bill, Herbie took a liking to the band, which reawakened his love for Brazilian music. Herbie recalled:

> The New York Samba Band had Romero Lubambo on guitar, Mark Soskin on keyboards, Paul Socolow on bass, and Duduka Da Fonseca on drums. When I heard them, I hired the whole band as my band. I should have done that five years earlier. For the first time in years, I went back to Brazil. And there were all these new writers: Ivan Lins, Djavan, Dori Caymmi, the post-Jobim evolution of young writers.

Romero Lubambo recalled:

> From then on, I started playing with Herbie and I never stopped.

There were some shows I could not do because I had other projects going on, but most of the gigs I did with him until the year that he died. When I met him, he was playing something completely different, more of a funky thing, but I remember that when he saw our band playing, he said, "Oh my god, that's the type of music I like"; and when he started using us, he started having fun again with Brazilian jazz. *Jasil Brazz* was the first album that we did together and it was a very beautiful record. We recorded at the Nola Studios in New York. There is a very popular drink in Brazil called caipirinha. It's made out of lime juice and a liquor called *cachaça*, which is made from sugarcane. I remember that Herbie brought everything necessary to make caipirinhas to the studio, so half of the album is beautiful ballads.

Nola, coincidentally or not, was the same studio where Herbie made his first records with Carmen McRae more than thirty-five years earlier for the Stardust label, although the studio by that time had moved down the block. Herbie didn't know it at the time, but the music he recorded on *Jasil Brazz* was at the forefront of a new kind of accessible jazz that radio stations labeled "smooth jazz." More melodically based than its mainstream cousin, smooth jazz was less challenging for non-jazz-oriented listeners to get accustomed to, consisting of softer sounds, more structured arrangements, and often using synthesizers and electronic keyboards. Smooth jazz artists such as Chris Botti and Dave Grusin became top sellers during the eighties and nineties, and Herbie's new Brazilian sound fit right into this mold.

In 1990, Herbie recorded another album of Latin-flavored easy listening jazz with Lubambo's group for the Chesky label, titled *Caminho de Casa*. That same year, he joined forces with fellow flutist Dave Valentin for five duets on Valentin's album *Two Amigos*, issued on Grusin and partner Larry Rosen's GRP label. *Two Amigos* would be the last album Herbie would make for a major label.

Now living in Santa Fe with Janeal and becoming acquainted with a new stable of Brazilian songwriters, Herbie was not only happy, but also more physically fit than at any time in his life. Herbie and Janeal actually produced an exercise video, *Get Fit to Herbie Mann & Janeal Arison & Friends*, issued in 1991.

Lubambo recalled:

> Sometimes we'd be driving and he'd go miles out of his way just
> to find something special that he really liked to eat. He liked to play
> places that were very beautiful. For example, we played in Hawaii
> seven times. He would bring the band and book the best hotel and
> make sure the promoters had the most comfortable places for us. He
> knew how to live well. We got to be like a family, all of us. I became
> almost like a son to him. His birthday was the same as my father's,
> so I had a father in Brazil and a father here in America.
>
> We trusted each other a lot and loved the same kind of music.
> He always gave me a lot of freedom on the stage; not only me, but
> the whole band. He was always looking for different things to play
> and never stopped being curious about new music. Herbie was very
> smart and very sensitive.

Herbie's return to Brazilian music was like a homecoming to him. The
disco years and the struggles to appease an intransigent, bottom-line-
oriented record company receded into the past, and his demeanor became
calmer and more philosophical. Herbie remembered:

> I discovered that anytime I get depressed, all I have to do is put
> on some Brazilian music, and it just lifts me up. We did *Jasil Brazz* for
> a label called the Moss Music Group. Then in 1989 I did an album
> called *Opalescence*, which was another Brazilian record that I made
> for a label called Gaia. Both of those companies went Chapter 11,
> so I got the masters back.
>
> Then I decided it was time to see if I could do it myself. So I
> formed Kokopelli Records. Kokopelli is the Indian god of fertility in
> the Southwest. He was the shaman who played the flute and walked
> around and got hired when there was no rain so that the crops would
> grow. While the farmers were out in the field, he was also taking care
> of their wives, so he was a bit of a trickster, too. Considering my past,
> I thought it was an apt name for the label. It was kind of a low-key
> operation out of the garage. I went to all of the musicians I knew
> who didn't have record contracts—Les McCann, Roy Ayers, David

Newman—and asked them if they'd like to do a co-op record. And we did *Deep Pocket*.

The idea was based on the fact distributors don't like to deal with a record company that has one artist and one record. So I came up with this idea. I said to myself, "How do I create a demand?" Normally, you hire a radio promotion man after the record comes out and gets in the stores. So I did a complete flip. I hired a promotion man to promote the records. Then the customers would call the radio station and say, "Where do we get the record?" Then the stores would call the radio stations and say, "How do we get this record?" So I went about it that way. There was a Tower Records store somewhere in Phoenix that contacted me, so I called Tower Records' offices and got them to be my distributor for *Deep Pocket*.

In 1992, *Deep Pocket* became the first release on the Kokopelli label. Herbie's business partner was Jim Geisler, an expansive wheeler-dealer Texan. *Deep Pocket* was typical Herbie: jazz-flavored versions of familiar charting pop tunes that leaned toward R&B and soul, such as the Temptations' "Papa Was a Rolling Stone," Wilson Pickett's "Mustang Sally," and Bobby Hebb's "Sunny." All the musicians on the record had played with Herbie at one time or another during his career: Les McCann on piano, David "Fathead" Newman on tenor sax, Roy Ayers on vibes, Richard Tee on keyboards, Cornell Dupree on electric guitar, Chuck Rainey on bass, and Buddy Williams on drums.

Other artists recorded for Kokopelli over the next five years, including pianist Jimmy Rowles, singer Sarah Vaughan, and newcomer composer Steve Barta, but the bulk of the releases were by a new crop of Brazilian jazz artists: Tania Maria, Ricardo Silveira, Brasilia, and Trio da Paz, the last consisting of Romero Lubambo, drummer Duduka Da Fonseca, and bassist Nilson Matta. Lubambo recalled the origins of Trio da Paz:

We just started playing in Duduka's basement. We were three Brazilians in New York, and at that time, I had a lot of time on my hands, so we started playing together in Duduka's house just for fun. Trio da Paz was created just like that. Later, we traveled a lot together with Herbie for I don't know how many years.

Sometime in the early 1990s, Herbie met Marty and Jay Ashby, two brothers who in 1987 helped start the Manchester Craftsmen's Guild (aka MCG Jazz), an organization devoted to preserving, presenting, and promoting jazz. Located in Pittsburgh, MCG Jazz was centered around an arts and mentoring school for inner-city youth, but also sponsored concerts and produced recordings on its own label. In addition to his role as executive producer for MCG Jazz, Marty Ashby was also an accomplished guitarist, while Jay played a variety of instruments, including trombone, saxophone, and percussion. Marty recalled:

> My brother Jay played in Astrud Gilberto's band for fifteen years, so he was kind of on the Brazilian circuit where Herbie was and they were in the same places a lot. In the early nineties, we had Herbie come up and play in our concert series. I think he had *Jasil Brazz* the first time he was here at the Guild. And he fell in love with the place in terms of the concept of what the school was all about and what we were trying to do with the training of adults and kids. So he just embraced the concept, and we became friends immediately. As a musician myself, that made it a little easier, but we really hit it off.

Herbie started working MCG Jazz events into his schedule, and he and the Ashbys found themselves working together whenever their schedules coincided. Of course, after getting to know Herbie, Marty Ashby soon became acquainted with Herbie's incessant passion for hockey and the New York Rangers.

> I knew he was a big hockey fan and a big Rangers fan. In the old days, we'd have concerts for five or six days in a row, but Herbie would come out before and do some workshops for Duquesne University. He played with the Duquesne Jazz Orchestra and then do his shows here at the guild. So he'd be in town with us for a week and we'd just hang out. I hooked it up for him to play "The Star-Spangled Banner" at a Pittsburgh Penguins game. As fate would have it, they were playing the Rangers. They made him a Penguins jersey that said "Mann" on the back of it. The next night, he wore that onstage at the concert hall and people went nuts.

Of course, during the game, we were in the owner's box watching the game. This was when Mario Lemieux was playing. Herbie finishes "The Star-Spangled Banner," and you know how it is at these hockey games, you're barely done with the last note and the guys are already on the ice. He finishes the song and Mario Lemieux just flies right by him on the ice.

Herbie and I then went up to the owner's box to watch the game . . . and he wouldn't shut up about the Rangers. At one point, I took him aside and just said, "Herbie, man, would you be cool about the Rangers?" We're there in the Penguins' owner's box and here he is, going on about the Rangers. But he didn't care. He was a Rangers fan and that was it. That's all that mattered.

In April 1995, Herbie celebrated his sixty-fifth birthday with a week's worth of performances at the Blue Note in New York City. He invited musicians from his past and present bands to join him for the nightly concerts. He remembered that week fondly:

That week was a very powerful experience for me. Not only did I experience a kaleidoscopic retrospective of my long musical life, but I was poignantly reminded of the deep love and respect that I share with so many of my musical brothers. It was quite an extraordinary week.

The lineup was like a who's who of jazz, with a different group playing each night. Michael Olatunji came with his African drums. Ray Mantilla, from the *Common Ground* band, played Afro-Cuban jazz, joined by guest artist Tito Puente on timbales. Others who joined the festivities included David Newman, Dave Valentin, Randy Brecker, Paquito D'Rivera, Victor Lewis, and Ron Carter. Herbie played an explosive nine-minute version of "Jungle Fantasy" and also performed Miles Davis's "All Blues," "Memphis Underground," and songs from "African Suite." The concerts were issued on two CDs, one titled *America/Brazil* and the other *Celebration*, both of which were issued on the Lightyear label.

Herbie issued only three CDs under his own name on Kokopelli; the first two were *Deep Pocket* and a reissue of *Opalescence*, the Gaia release from

1989. But the most satisfying album of them all was *Peace Pieces*, the tribute to Bill Evans that Herbie had yearned to do ever since being intimidated by Evans's presence during the 1961 *Nirvana* session for Atlantic. Evans had died in 1980, but in 1995, Herbie was ready to try again. He recalled:

> I wanted to do a straight-ahead album. And I wanted to do a whole album of Bill Evans's music. I spent four or five months working on the record, because I wanted to make sure that I wouldn't be ashamed of it this time. I was very happy with the results. My two favorite songs on the album were arranged by Bob Freedman, "Blue in Green" and "Peace Piece," which were written for flute choir: four C flutes, four alto flutes, and bass flute, and I played all the parts.

Herbie wisely chose not to include a piano on the record, but it wasn't necessary. The album, highlighted by the two flute choir arrangements, was one of the most elegant and satisfying of his career. The liner photo showed an elegant, sophisticated Herbie, dressed in a stark white suit, with his flute lying on the top of a black grand piano. In the album notes, Herbie said, "It's said that we bring to our lives what we need when we need it. I think that the process of doing this project has been a very important and timely gift to my life. It demanded a deeper level of understanding and a more disciplined command of my instrument than I have been previously willing to risk. The result has been deeply gratifying and has provided me with a new standard."

Like every other challenge during his career, Herbie met the disappointment with his first album of Bill Evans tunes head-on, which resulted in one of the finest albums of his career. But in 1997, a bigger, more devastating challenge presented itself, which resulted in Herbie spending the next six years fighting for his life.

27

BEYOND BROOKLYN

In 1997, Herbie and partner Jim Geisler decided to end their relationship as partners in Kokopelli. Herbie later recalled:

> It was like living in a white tower. I didn't watch the business. So then it went south. I separated from him, got back all my masters, and then worked out a deal with Lightyear, which was a label distributed by Warner Bros., to release the live recordings of my sixty-fifth birthday at the Blue Note, and they also rereleased the *Peace Pieces* album.

The previous fall, Herbie noticed he was starting to have issues with impotence. His wife Janeal recalled:

> Sex was a big part of our life. We were a really sexy couple. [*Laughs*] He was twenty-two years older than me and I was a hot, young woman. So he went to a urologist and the doctor gave him testosterone. My stepfather had had prostate cancer so he suggested Herbie get a PSA test. Herbie took the test and it was off the charts, something like a 14.9. I'll never forget the phone call he got from the doctor. He said, "You need to come in for a biopsy." After that, we went to another doctor, and I remember waiting in the waiting room for him and when he came out, the doctor said, "Well, there's no need for surgery," and we both went "Whew!" because we thought

it was all right. But it wasn't all right. It was inoperable. The cancer was already out of the seminal vesicles and had spread. They caught it too late.

We went to Sloan-Kettering in New York for three months of radiation, and then it was six years of going back and forth, getting chemotherapy. Herbie was all about turning lemons into lemonade so we formed the Prostate Cancer Awareness Foundation. We had learned something really important: that early detection is the best way to beat prostate cancer. So we went out and spoke. Herbie would play concerts and have on-site PSA tests given. And he would offer a free CD to anyone who took the test. We produced quite a few of these concerts. Herbie became a spokesperson for prostate cancer awareness. He participated in the first universal march against prostate cancer in Washington, D.C., which was led by Norman Schwarzkopf. Herbie played "America the Beautiful" right after Jesse Jackson spoke, right on the grounds of the Washington Monument. He was genuinely committed to that cause.

In 1999, Herbie said:

When all of a sudden you realize that you're not going to live forever, you start looking at your life and looking at what you want to be remembered for. So it dawned on me that my whole life I have played music that I have loved that wasn't really my heritage. I'm not Cuban, I'm not Brazilian, I'm not Jamaican, I'm not black, I'm not Middle Eastern. I'm an Eastern European Jew. And I had been writing all this music and putting it away because I never thought it belonged. They were all sad Russian and Romanian kinds of songs. So I thought, "Why don't I just go there now?"

The following April, Herbie and Janeal went to Budapest, where they met musicians who were also rediscovering their own musical traditions. Throughout his long and varied career, Herbie had never been to Eastern Europe. He later recalled having an eerie, indescribable feeling of having come home. The album *Eastern European Roots* was recorded in the spring and summer of 2000.

The session was held at the Stepbridge Studios in Santa Fe. Most of the songs were written by Herbie, beautifully melodic compositions that sounded simultaneously sad and nostalgic. There were dance tunes and melancholy tunes, and on "A Dance at the Rise of the Moon," Geoff Mann showed he had inherited his father's knack for melody with a wonderfully atmospheric and lively composition of his own. Herbie was understandably proud to record with his son, and his own effervescent playing on the number was as inventive as it had ever been. The old excitement was back.

One of the songs, "Jelek," was written by Hungarian saxophonist Mihály Borbély and recorded in Hungary with Borbély's own jazz quartet. For the band, which he called Sona Terra ("songs of the earth"), Herbie brought out the old shepherd's flute he had played on "The Evolution of Mann." Sona Terra included Gil Goldstein on accordion, Alexander Fedoriouk on cimbalom, Bruce Dunlap on guitar, Paul Socolow on bass, and Herbie's son Geoff on drums. A photograph of a proud Herbie with his ninety-five-year-old mother, Ruth, born in Romania in 1905, graced the inside of the CD. Proceeds from the album's sales went to support prostate cancer awareness.

In 2000, Herbie recorded several tracks for an MCG Jazz Christmas album by singer Nancy Wilson. An all-star lineup of performers joined Wilson on the session, including Paquito D'Rivera, Bill Watrous, Gary Burton, James Moody, Jimmy Heath, and many others. At the time, Herbie was living in Santa Fe and was still relatively healthy. Marty Ashby flew out to Santa Fe and recorded Herbie playing two solos for the album, including a memorable version of "White Christmas" on alto flute.

That year, another CD came out of a concert Herbie played in July 1998 at the Standard Bank National Youth Jazz Festival in Grahamstown, South Africa. Titled *African Mann*, the CD came out in 2000 on the Chord label as an import but had very poor distribution and did not sell well.

At MCG Jazz's fifteenth anniversary concert in April 2002, Herbie played a benefit for prostate cancer awareness with Brazilian guitarist Oscar Castro-Neves, Herbie's old Brooklyn friend Phil Woods, Hendrik Meurkens, and others. Marty Ashby recalled, "That concert went so well that we decided to make a recording. Herbie and Phil went back in time to when they would play for a bowl of pasta in Brooklyn jam sessions."

The album was recorded in November 2002 and called *Beyond Brooklyn*. It turned out to be the last album Herbie ever made. Phil Woods recalled:

Manchester Craftsmen's Guild called me. It was their idea, Marty and Jay Ashby. They knew about *Yardbird Suite* and our Brooklyn days, and I'm sure glad we did it. We had a ball on that last album. That was a joyous occasion. Herbie was in one isolation booth and I was in another, but we had a great time just yelling in the microphone at each other. Playing with him again was a joy, a real joy. We went back to our Brooklyn roots. I brought in a couple of songs, Herbie picked a couple, and the Ashby brothers picked a couple. I don't think he'd played much bebop before then, but he sounded darned good. He could still swing it.

He was not feeling too great, though. I was downstairs with my oxygen machine and he was in a wheelchair. We were both huffing and puffing a little bit, but my ailments were not as severe as his. Unfortunately, he didn't last much longer. That was his last outing.

28

THE LAST HILL

The last year of Herbie's life was very difficult, as he fought bravely but helplessly against the disease. In interviews, he was philosophical:

> The beginning of my career was like the first hill of the roller coaster. There were incredible highs and incredible lows. Now, it's like those little hills at the end of the roller coaster. They go up, they go down, they go up, they go down. And by this time, that was OK.

But Herbie was hiding his true feelings about dealing with the ultimate end of his life. His wife Janeal said:

> Herbie was pissed. He was so angry that he was dying. He really was furious. He really didn't want to go. And sometimes he got a little nasty about it. That was hard to deal with from my perspective, but who could blame him?

On April 16, 2003, Herbie turned seventy-three years old. He and Janeal invited about a hundred friends to their home in Santa Fe for what was being called "Herbie's Going Away Party." It was basically a chance for all of his friends to come and tell him good-bye. It was a very emotional time for all, and although there was a lot of kidding around and denials that Herbie was going anywhere, Herbie knew his time wasn't long and wanted to take care of a few final things while he was still able to. One of these was to appear at the New Orleans Jazz Heritage Festival, which took place every May. Janeal recalled:

> Normally, Herbie never practiced his flute at home. Ever. *Ever.* Except when he was dying. For that last album with Phil Woods, he practiced a lot for that, and it really showed. The other album he practiced for was *Peace Pieces*. That was the album where he really was trying to claim his ground as a flutist. Bill Evans was his very favorite piano player. We were in Carefree, Arizona, and he felt a spurt of energy and thought that maybe he should be in a lower altitude, so I found us a house to rent. By then he was on oxygen pretty much half the time. He knew this New Orleans gig was coming up on May the third and wanted to get his chops together for that. So we rented this house, and for a month and a half, we stayed there and he practiced.
>
> Then we went to the New Orleans Festival. And that was a challenge because he had to go in a wheelchair with an oxygen tank with him. I had to carry the oxygen onstage for him because he was so weak.
>
> There was a huge crowd in New Orleans, and it was hot and humid in the tent where he was playing. I don't think anyone left that tent the same as when they came in, because it was quite an extraordinary thing to watch him play. You could just see that he was acknowledging the audience and the life that he had lived. He wasn't in too much pain and got through it nobly and fairly gracefully, but he was not happy with his performance.

Herbie's band included Ricky Sebastian, Chuck Rainey, Larry Coryell, David Newman, and Mark Soskin. At the end of the show, they all stood, arm in arm, and saluted and waved to the cheering audience of five thousand fans, many of whom had tears in their eyes. Herbie, wearing a colorful Hawaiian shirt, but drawn and obviously tired, got up also to acknowledge the crowd.

A few weeks later, he went to Phoenix, Arizona, with the Ashbys to complete some overdubs for the *Beyond Brooklyn* album at Glen Campbell's home studio. According to Marty Ashby:

By that time, Herbie had gotten really sick. My brother Jay was in Paul Simon's band, so that's how we got Glen Campbell's studio, through his road manager. It was a very powerful session. He was on oxygen half the time, and Janeal was in the booth with him the entire time while he was doing overdubs. When we finished, Herbie said, "I want to play one more song." Jay and I said, "Well, we didn't bring any instruments with us." We were just there to do a couple of flute fixes to finish the record. But Herbie insisted, "I've got to play 'Time After Time' [a 1947 song written by Sammy Cahn and Jule Styne that was popularized by Frank Sinatra] for Janeal. It's our song and I have to play it for her." So the engineer let us into Glen Campbell's house and I got Glen's guitar. Jay had a little egg shaker in his bag, and we found a floor tom, which sounds like a Brazilian *sordu*, and we recorded an instantaneous, on-the-spot arrangement of "Time After Time." The words to that are very powerful. Even though Herbie was very ill by this point, he created a vibrant, courageous, and loving sound that could have been recorded thirty years earlier.

And we did it in one take. I had to go outside afterwards because it was so beautiful but also so very sad. We had been in the studio for four or five hours, but when we got outside in the sun, it was an absolutely beautiful Phoenix day. Eighty-five degrees, and gorgeous. It was very refreshing to have the sun hit us all. Then Herbie came out and we took a photo of the three of us. That was the last time I ever saw him.

When the session was over, Janeal took Herbie home. She recalled his last days:

We went to our home in Pecos, which he loved. It was a great place for him to be. One of the things I'm really proud of is that I gave him as good a death as one person could have. For the last six months of his life, I did nothing but take care of him. There weren't any other people around because he didn't want anyone around. He got to die in our bed. When I saw it coming, I got hospice to come help out. He loved being in the country. We got all of his kids there except Paul, who just really couldn't bring himself to come. The others all came out, and Herbie held on until they got there.

Herbie Mann died shortly before midnight on July 1, 2003, with his family by his side. He was seventy-three. According to his wishes, his body was cremated. Before his death, Herbie and Janeal decided to bequeath all of his memorabilia to the Manchester Craftsmen's Guild, where it now resides.

On October 23, 2003, a memorial service was held at St. Peter's Church in New York City. Speakers included Ahmet Ertegun and Herbie's close friend Sy Johnson, while performers included Marcus Johnson, Phil Travis, Buddy Williams, and Bobbi Humphrey.

29

CODA

When I interviewed Herbie in 1999, it was clear he was looking at the end of his life, although at the time he was feeling well and wasn't yet suffering excessively from the symptoms of his disease. I asked him about his legacy and what he thought he would be remembered for.

> The flute was something that everybody said couldn't happen. Brazilian music was something everybody said wouldn't happen. "World music" was some little bin in the record store. I think the musicians now, their vocabulary incorporates a lot broader spectrum than it did in the fifties and sixties. I think that there are people who are more tolerant of more different music forms than before. And I think I had a part in that.

Herbie's mother, Ruth, outlived her son by more than a year. She died in November 2004 at the age of ninety-nine. After Herbie's death, Janeal married Aaron Jones, a successful artist, photographer, and cinematographer. She has faced her own battles with cancer, but has attacked the disease with the same grace and fortitude Herbie did.

On July 3, 2009, Herbie's oldest son, Paul, died in an accident on the Columbia River in Hood River, Oregon. He was forty-eight. His sister Claudia recalled:

> Paul was the smartest person I ever knew. He was well read, he

was well traveled, but he had epileptic seizures occasionally but didn't want anyone to know he was having them. He refused to take medication because they take away your driver's license for a few days so they can see how you're doing and he didn't want to go through that. Anyway, he was paddling on one of those paddleboards and wasn't wearing a life vest or even an ankle strap. That was Paul. The river was calm like glass, and all of a sudden, he disappeared. It took three days to find him.

Herbie Mann was not only the first jazz musician to specialize on the flute, but is also recognized by many as being the most popular, successful, versatile, and honored musician on the instrument as well. When asked about this, Herbie characteristically but modestly took credit where credit was due:

> There certainly are people that are more talented than me, but as far as popular, probably. My wish all along was to be as synonymous with the flute as Benny Goodman was with the clarinet. And I think I've done that.

In the life of a professional musician, the endless string of gigs, record dates, and jam sessions normally blur together, but occasionally, one stands out from all the others. For Marty Ashby, it was a show he played with Herbie Mann.

> I didn't play with Herbie very many times over the years because he used Romero all the time on guitar. But on one particular gig, it was an afternoon performance that I will never forget. The thing about Herbie is that he always expected to have a great performance, whether it was at the Hollywood Bowl or for two hundred people in the mountains of Pennsylvania.
>
> We played one set. There was something from the Bill Evans album and a potpourri of some Brazilian and some straight-ahead songs. Maybe six tunes in all. When it was over, everybody on the bandstand knew that we had done something very special. Everybody took perfect solos. Herbie was great and his playing was

just amazing. The energy just built from one tune to the next. We finished the set, and all of our mouths hung open. We had had a musical orgasm that was unbelievable, and we all knew it. Herbie turned around and said to everyone, "That was nice, fellas. Let's go eat." And then he bought everybody dinner. Like he always did.

List of Sources

Books

Bennett, Tony. *The Good Life*. New York: Pocket Books, 1998.

Feld, Steven. *Jazz Cosmopolitanism in Accra: Five Musical Years in Ghana*. Durham: Duke University Press Books, 2012.

Gioia, Ted. *West Coast Jazz*. New York: Oxford University Press, 1992.

Houghton, Mick. *Becoming Elektra: The True Story of Jac Holzman's Visionary Record Label*. London: Jawbone Press, 2010.

James, Billy. *Necessity Is: The Early Years of Frank Zappa and the Mothers of Invention*, London: SAF Publishing Ltd., 2001.

Kanfer, Stefan. *Stardust Lost: The Triumph, Tragedy, and Mishugas of the Yiddish Theater in America*. New York: Alfred A. Knopf, 2006.

Maggin, Donald L. *Dizzy: The Life and Times of John Birks Gillespie*, New York: HarperCollins Publishers, 2005.

Mazzoletti, Adriano. *Il Jazz in Italia, Volume 2*, Italy: EDT, 2010.

Monson, Ingrid. *Freedom Sounds: Civil Rights Call Out to Jazz and Africa*. New York: Oxford University Press, 2007.

Olatunji, Babatunde with Robert Atkinson. *The Beat of My Drum: An Autobiography*, Philadelphia: Temple University Press, 2005.

Poe, Randy. *Skydog: The Duane Allman Story*. New York: Backbeat Books, 2006.

Ruppli, Michel, with Bob Porter. *The Savoy Label: A Discography*. Westport: Greenwood Press, 1980.

Shipton, Alyn. *Groovin' High: The Life of Dizzy Gillespie*, New York: Oxford University Press, 1999.

Umphred, Neal. *Goldmine's Price Guide to Collectible Jazz Albums: 1949-1969*, Iola: Krause Publications, 1994.

Westbrook, Peter. *The Flute in Jazz: Window on World Music*. Rockville: Harmonia Books, 2011.

Yanow, Scott. *Jazz on Record: The First Sixty Years*. San Francisco: Back Beat Books, 2003.

Articles, Periodicals, and Blogs

Note: Many articles in music trade magazines were consulted for this book, especially those of DownBeat *and* Billboard. *Significant articles used are listed below.*

Blumenthal, Bob. "Herbie Mann and His Unfortunate 'Family'," *Philadelphia After Dark*, February 4, 1970, p. 5.

"Bossa Nova," *Time*, September 21, 1962.

Ellison, Bob. "The World and Herbie Mann," *DownBeat*, August 27, 1964, pp. 13-14.

"Embryo Shifts Disk Course — Mann Plans Seven Albums," *Billboard*, October 17, 1970, p. 3.

"Family Legacy Endures: Mother of Herbie Mann Dancing at 98," *SunSentinel*, September 10, 2003.

Feather, Leonard. "Herbie Mann's Many Record Faces," *Los Angeles Times Calendar*, January 4, 1970, p. 36.

_____ & Howard Mandel. "Herbie Mann's Independent Flute and the Blues," *DownBeat*, December 1980, pp. 20-21, 56-57.

Friedwald, Will. "Recording Jazz History as It Was Made," *The Wall Street Journal*, December 4, 2010.

Gitler, Ira. "The Family of Mann," *DownBeat*, November 28, 1968, pp. 15-17.

"Herbie Mann Forms Embryo Label," *Record World*, June 6, 1970.

"Jazz in the Jungle," *Time*, March 28, 1960.

"Jazz: The Third Thing," *Time*, December 18, 1964.

McKenna, Julie. "Herbie Mann: Jazz Flutist and Prostate Cancer Survivor," *Coping with Cancer*, November/December 2001.

Myers, Mark. "A. K. Salim: Flute Suite," *Jazz Wax*, December 23, 2008.

Nelsen, Don. "Herbie Mann His Own Man," *New York Daily News*, May 13, 1978.

Schrieber, Norman. "Herbie Mann with Twenty Hot Albums to His Credit Won't Let Himself Just Settle Down," *Sir*, 1966.

Tiegel, Eliot. "Herbie Mann: Going Through Some Changes," *Jazz & Pop*, January 1971, pp. 25-26.

Willard, Patricia. "The Essence of Mann," *DownBeat*, October 10, 1974.

Album Notes

All albums by Herbie Mann unless otherwise specified

Altshuler, Bob. *My Kinda Groove*. Atlantic 1433 (1965).

Anonymous. *Herbie Mann with the Wessel Ilcken Trio*. Epic LN-3499 (1958).

_____ *Hi-Flutin'*. Premier PS-2001 (1957).

_____ *Moods* (Paul Quinichette). EmArcy MG-36003 (1955).

_____ *Scotch on the Rocks* (Joe Saye). EmArcy MG-36072 (1956).

Becker, Gene. *Rugolomania* (Pete Rugolo). Columbia CL-689 (1955).

Bennett, Al. *Glory of Love*. A&M SP-3003 (1967).

Berendt, Joachim E. *Concerto Grosso in D Blues*. Atlantic SD-1540 (1969).

Conover, Willis. *Herbie Mann at the Village Gate*. Atlantic 1380 (1962).

_____ *Herbie Mann Live at Newport*. Atlantic 1413 (1963).

_____ Jazz Committee for Latin American Affairs (Various Artists). FM FSR-704 (1963).

D'Lugoff, Art. *Monday Night at the Village Gate*. Atlantic 1462 (1966).

Feather, Leonard. *The Evolution of Mann*. Atlantic SD 2-300 (1972).

_____ *Flautista: Herbie Mann Plays Afro-Cuban Jazz*. Verve MG V-8336 (1959).

_____ *Flute, Brass, Vibes & Percussion*. Verve V6-8392 (1961).

_____ *Jazz Studio 5* (Ralph Burns & His Orchestra). Decca DL-8235 (1956)

_____ *Latin Mann*. Columbia CS-9188 (1965).

_____ *New Mann at Newport*. Atlantic SD-1471 (1967).

_____ *Winter Sequence* (Leonard Feather & Ralph Burns). M-G-M E-270 (1954)

Frazier, George. *Turtle Bay*. Atlantic SD-1642 (1973).

Gitler, Ira. *Orgy in Rhythm* (Art Blakey). Blue Note BLP-1554/1555 (1957).

_____ *Trust in Me* (Soul Flutes). A&M SP-3009 (1968).

Gold, Don. *The Family of Mann*. Atlantic 1371 (1961).

Green, Stanley. *This Is My Beloved* (Laurence Harvey). Atlantic 1367 (1962).

Halman, Talat S. *Impressions of the Middle East*. Atlantic SD-1475 (1967).

Hentoff, Nat. *The Magic Flute of Herbie Mann*. Verve MG V-8247 (1957).

_____ *Salute to the Flute*. Epic LN-3395 (1957).

Johnson, Sy. *The Evolution of Mann*. Rhino R2-71634 (1994).

Katzell, Bud. *Machito with Flute to Boot* (Machito & His Afro-Cuban Jazz Ensemble). Roulette R-52026 (1959).

Keepnews, Orrin. *Billy Taylor with Four Flutes* (Billy Taylor). Riverside RLP-1151 (1959)

Korall, Burt. *Music For Suburban Living* (New York Quartet). Coral CRL-57136 (1958)

Kraft, Lee. *New York Jazz Quartet*. Elektra EKL-115 (1957).

Laredo, Joseph F. *The Herbie Mann — Sam Most Quintet*. Bethlehem/Avenue Jazz R275731 (1956).

Lees, Gene. *Big Boss Mann*. Columbia CS-1068 (1973).

Levy, Arthur. *Gagaku & Beyond*. Finnadar SR-9014 (1976).

_____ *Surprises*. Atlantic SD-1682 (1976).

Maher, Jack. *Herbie Mann Returns to the Village Gate*. Atlantic 1407 (1963).

Mann, Herbie. *Brazil, Bossa Nova & Blues*. United Artists UAJ-14009 (1962).

_____ *The Common Ground*. Atlantic 1343 (1960).

_____ *East Coast Jazz/4*. Bethlehem BCP-1018 (1954).

_____ *Flamingo* (The Herbie Mann Quartet). Bethlehem BCP-24 (1955).

Neely, Hal. *The Epitome of Jazz*. Bethlehem BCP-6067 (1961).

New York Jazz Quartet. *The New York Jazz Quartet Goes Native* (New York Jazz Quartet). Elektra EKL-118 (1957).

Quinn, Joe. *Herbie Mann — Sam Most Quintet.* Bethlehem BCP-40 (1956).

_____ *Love and the Weather.* Bethlehem BCP-63 (1956).

Ramsey, Doug. *The Mann with the Most,* the Herbie Mann/Sam Most Quintet. Bethlehem BCP-6020 (LP reissue).

Rolontz, Bob. *A Mann and A Woman* (Herbie Mann & Tamiko Jones). Atlantic 8141 (1967).

_____ *Today.* Atlantic 1454 (1966).

Shapiro, Nat. *A Musical Offering* (Don Elliott Sextette). ABC-Paramount ABC-106 (1956).

_____ *Legrand Jazz* (Michel Legrand). Columbia CL-1250 (1958).

Shaw, Arnold. *The Beat Goes On.* Atlantic SD-1483 (1967).

Siders, Harvey. *Et Tu Flute.* Verve 2-V6S-8821 (1973).

Simon, Bill. *Carmen McRae* (Carmen McRae with the Mat Mathews Quartet). Bethlehem BCP-1023 (1955).

Simon, George T. *Mat Mathews.* Brunswick BL 54013, 1954.

_____ *Right Now.* Atlantic 1384 (1962).

_____ *Standing Ovation at Newport.* Atlantic 1445 (1966).

Stein, H. Alan. *Flute Suite* (A. K. Salim). Savoy MG-12102 (1957).

Stein, H. Alan. *Mann Alone.* Savoy MG-12107 (1957).

Torin, "Symphony Sid." *Herbie Mann's African Suite.* United Artists UAS-5042 (1959).

Various. *Hommage à Nesuhi.* Atlantic Records (special-edition box set) RHM2-7760 (2008).

Interviews

Herbie Mann — phone interview: April 4, 1995; Hollywood, California: June 19, 1995; Santa Fe, New Mexico: November 30—December 1, 1999.

Janeal Arison — Beverly Hills, California: July 14, 2013.

Marty Ashby — phone interview: October 3, 2013.

Ray Barretto — phone interview: February 18, 2000.

Béhague, Gerard — phone interview: February 4, 2000.

Buddy Collette — Studio City, California: April 17, 1995.

Judi Solomon Kennedy — phone interview: April 25, 2013.

List of Sources

John Levy — Pasadena, California: February 10, 2000.
Mundell Lowe — phone interview: July 5, 2013.
Romero Lubambo — September 24, 2013
Claudia Mann — phone interview: August 15, 2013.
Ray Mantilla — phone interview: June 23, 2013.
Arif Mardin — phone interview: February 29, 2000.
Sam Most — Tarzana, California: April 29, 2012.
Dave Pike — phone interview: August 29, 2013.
Phil Woods — phone interview: August 29, 2013.

Selected Discography

Herbie Mann's recording career consisted of recordings he made under his own name as well as numerous appearances as a sideman, especially in the 1950s. This selected discography is divided into two sections, which focuses chiefly on long-playing vinyl albums and CDs, but also includes 78 and 45 rpm singles that did not appear on albums.

Since there have been a significant number of reissues and repackaging of Herbie Mann's recordings, I have only listed the titles of original releases. In the second section, I have included the names of artists Herbie recorded with and their respective labels.

A comprehensive discography of all recordings featuring Herbie Mann is being completed for separate publication.

RECORDINGS BY HERBIE MANN

1954: *Herbie Mann Plays* (Bethlehem — 10-inch LP)

1955: *Flamingo* (aka *Volume 2*) (Bethlehem), *For Flute Lovers* (with Sam Most) (Bethlehem), *Herbie Mann Plays* (Bethlehem).

1956: *Love and the Weather* (Bethlehem), *Historic Jazz Concert at Music Inn* (Atlantic — one track), *Mann in the Morning* (Prestige), *Herbie Mann with the Wessel Ilcken Trio* (Epic).

1957: *Flute Soufflé* (with Bobby Jasper) (Prestige), *Sultry Serenade* (Riverside), *Salute to the Flute* (Epic), *Mann Alone* (Savoy), *Yardbird Suite* (Savoy), *Great Ideas of Western Mann* (Riverside), *Flute Fraternity* (Mode), *The Magic Flute of Herbie Mann* (Verve).

1958: *Just Wailin'* (with Charlie Rouse, Kenny Burrell, Mal Waldron) (New Jazz).

1959: *Flautista! Herbie Mann Plays Afro-Cuban Jazz* (Verve), *African Suite* (as Johnny Rae's Afro-Jazz Septet) (United Artists).

1960: *Flute, Brass, Vibes & Percussion* (Verve), *The Common Ground* (Atlantic), *Wailin' Modernist* (Alto).

1961: *The Family of Mann* (Atlantic), *Herbie Mann at the Village Gate* (Atlantic), *Herbie Mann Returns to the Village Gate* (Atlantic), *Nirvana* (with the Bill Evans Trio) (Atlantic).

1962: *Brazil, Bossa Nova & Blues* (United Artists), *Right Now* (Atlantic), *Do the Bossa Nova with Herbie Mann* (Atlantic), *Latin Fever* (Atlantic), *Herbie Mann & Joao Gilberto with Antonio Carlos Jobim* (Atlantic).

1963: *Herbie Mann Live at Newport* (Atlantic), *Our Mann Flute* (Atlantic), *My Kinda Groove* (Atlantic), *The Beat Goes On* (Atlantic).

1964: Unknown Title (ONS).

1965: *The Roar of the Greasepaint — The Smell of the Crowd* (Atlantic), *Standing Ovation at Newport* (Atlantic), *Latin Mann* (Columbia), *Today* (Atlantic).

1966: *Impressions of the Middle East* (Atlantic), *The Herbie Mann String Album* (Atlantic), *New Mann at Newport* (Atlantic), *A Mann and a Woman* (with Tamiko Jones) (Atlantic), *The Beat Goes On* (Atlantic).

1967: *The Wailing Dervishes* (Atlantic), *Glory of Love* (A&M), 45 rpm single with Carmen McRae (Atlantic).

1968: *Windows Opened* (Atlantic), *Trust in Me* (aka *Soul Flutes*) (A&M), *The Inspiration I Feel* (Atlantic), *Memphis Underground* (Atlantic), *Concerto Grosso in D Blues* (Atlantic).

1969: *Stone Flute* (Embryo), *Live at the Whisky a Go Go* (Atlantic), "It's a Funky Thing — Right On" 45 rpm single (Atlantic), *Muscle Shoals Nitty Gritty* (Embryo).

1970: *Memphis Two-Step* (Embryo).

1971: *Herbie Mann '71* (with Air — unreleased) (Embryo), *Push Push* (Embryo).

1972: *Mississippi Gambler* (Atlantic), *Mar y Sol: The First International Puerto Rico Pop Festival* (one track — Atco), *Hold On, I'm Comin'* (Atlantic).

1973: *Turtle Bay* (Atlantic), *London Underground* (Atlantic), *Reggae* (Atlantic), *Reggae II* (Atlantic — issued only in New Zealand), *The Family of Mann: First Light* (Atlantic).

1974: *Surprises* (Atlantic), *Gagaku & Beyond* (Finnadar).

1975: *Discothèque* (Atlantic), *Waterbed* (Atlantic), "The Stars and Stripes Forever" (45 rpm single — Atlantic).

1976: *Bird in a Silver Cage* (Atlantic).

1977: *Fire Island* (Atlantic).

1978: *Brazil Once Again* (Atlantic), *Super Mann* (Atlantic), (Atlantic), *Yellow Fever* (Atlantic).

1979: *Sunbelt* (Atlantic).

1980: *Herbie Mann Music* (Herbie Mann Music).

1981: *Mellow* (Atlantic).

1983: *Astral Island* (Atlantic).

1985: *See Through Spirits* (Atlantic).

1987: *Jasil Brazz* (RBI).

1989: *Opalescence* (Gaia).

1990: *Caminho de Casa* (Chesky).

1992: *Deep Pocket* (Kokopelli).

1995: *Peace Pieces* (Kokopelli).

1997: *65th Birthday Celebration* (Lightyear Entertainment), *America/Brazil* (Lightyear Entertainment).

1998: *African Mann* (Chord).

2000: *Eastern European Roots* (with Sona Terra) (Herbie Mann Music).

2001: *To Grover with Love* (one track, "Mr. Magic") (Artizen Music Group).

2002: *Beyond Brooklyn* (with Phil Woods) (MCG Jazz).

2003: "Time After Time" (MCG Jazz).

RECORDINGS FEATURING HERBIE MANN

Early 1953: Mat Mathews Quintet (Jubilee).

1953: Carmen McRae with the Mat Mathews Quintet (Stardust, Venus, Bethlehem), Mat Mathews Quintet (Brunswick).

1954: Leonard Feather, Ralph Burns & Their Orchestra (M-G-M), Pete Rugolo & His Orchestra (Columbia, Harmony), Paul Quinichette (EmArcy), Sarah Vaughan with the Clifford Brown Sextet (EmArcy).

1955: Quincy Jones & the All Stars (Columbia — one track), Chris Connor with Ralph Sharon (Bethlehem), Carmen McRae (Decca), Ralph Burns & His Orchestra (Decca), Terry Morel (Bethlehem),

Don Elliott Sextette (ABC-Paramount), Marlene VerPlanck (Savoy), Hank Jones (Savoy — one track).

1956: Bob Stewart with Mat Mathews' Quintet (Dawn), Tom Stewart Sextette/Quintette (ABC-Paramount), *Porgy & Bess* (Bethlehem), Howard McGhee Orchestra (Bethlehem), Frances Faye (Bethlehem), Joe Saye (EmArcy), Mat Mathews (Dawn & Jazztone), Boyd Raeburn & His Orchestra (Columbia), the Australian Jazz Quartet/Quintet (Bethlehem — 1 track), the Manhattan Jazz Septette (Coral), Joe Puma Sextet (Harmony, Concert Hall, Allegro), Don Elliott Septet (ABC-Paramount), Erroll Garner Trio (Columbia), Quincy Jones & His Orchestra (ABC-Paramount), Johnny Eaton (Columbia).

1957: The New York Jazz Quartet (Elektra, Coral), Chris Connor (Atlantic), Carol Stevens (Atlantic), the New York Jazz Ensemble (Elektra), Art Blakey Percussion Ensemble (Blue Note), A. K. Salim (Savoy), Jackie & Roy (ABC-Paramount), Lurlean Hunter (Vik), Joe Saye (EmArcy), Ella Mae Morse (Calliope), the Four Freshmen (Capitol), Tony Bennett (Columbia), Machito & His Orchestra (Roulette).

1958: Buddy DeFranco (Verve), Michel Legrand (Columbia), Machito & His Afro-Cuban Ensemble (Roulette), Johnny Pace (Riverside), Chet Baker Septet (Riverside).

1959: Chet Baker Septet (Riverside), Mundell Lowe & His All Stars (RCA Camden), Joe Wilder (Columbia), Philly Joe Jones Big Band (Riverside), Billy Taylor (Riverside), Beverly Kenney (Decca), Michel Legrand (Columbia).

1960: Count Basie (Roulette), Laurence Harvey (Atlantic).

1961: Jazz Committee for Latin American Affairs (Various Artists) (FM).

1962: Bobby Short (Atlantic), Lavern Baker (Atlantic).

1971: Air (Embryo).

1973: T-Bone Walker (Reprise).

1977: The Atlantic Family Live at Montreux (Atlantic), Narada Michael Walden (Atlantic), Klaus Doldinger (ACT).

1978: Jay McShann (Atlantic).

1979: The Bee Gees (RSO).

1986: Ornella Vanoni (CGD).

1988: Jeramzee (WEA).

1990: Dave Valentin (GRP).

1991: Steve Barta (Kokopelli).

1992: Trio da Paz (Concord Picante).

1994: Trio da Paz (Kokopelli).

1995: Steve Barta (Kokopelli — one track).

1996: Stereolab (Antilles/Verve), Jason Miles (Lightyear).

1998: Leviev-Slon & Co. (Elephant).

2001: Nancy Wilson (MCG Jazz).

2002: Romero Lubambo (FFO).

Index

Index

Hal Leonard
JAZZ BIOGRAPHY SERIES

WALK TALL
THE MUSIC AND LIFE OF JULIAN "CANNONBALL" ADDERLEY
by Cary Ginell
Foreword by Quincy Jones

Cannonball Adderley introduces his 1967 recording of "Walk Tall," by saying, "There are times when things don't lay the way they're supposed to lay. But regardless, you're supposed to hold your head up high and walk tall." This sums up the life of Julian "Cannonball" Adderley, a man who used a gargantuan technique on the alto saxophone, pride in heritage, devotion to educating youngsters, and insatiable musical curiosity to bridge gaps between jazz and popular music in the 1960s and '70s. Covering his early days through his untimely death at forty-six, *Walk Tall* is the captivating story of Cannonball's musical legacy.

978-1-4584-1979-8 ....$18.99

MR. B
THE MUSIC AND LIFE OF BILLY ECKSTINE
by Cary Ginell
Foreword by Ed Eckstein

Movie-star handsome with an elegant pencil-thin mustache and a wide vibrato, Billy Eckstine possessed one of the most magnificent voices in popular music history. Signing with MGM, he rose to superstar status, sold millions of records, marketed his own line of "Mr. B." shirt collars, and inspired an army of female admirers, known as "Billy-soxers." Eckstine fought all his life for recognition and respect in his quest to become America's first black romantic singing idol, but he faced hardships in the segregated music world of the '40s and '50s. *Mr. B.* examines the life of one of the twentieth century's most amazing success stories, from his early days in Pittsburgh to his time in Las Vegas.

978-1-4584-1980-4 ....$18.99

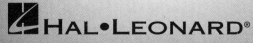

HAL•LEONARD®
halleonardbooks.com